MAFIA BOSS'S SURPRISE BABY

KIRA COLE

1

DANTE

I take a deep breath as I walk into my father's office. I haven't been in here since he died a couple of weeks ago, but I know that this is where all his important documents are. I'm looking for anything that might help me, really, although I'm really hoping to find his will.

My more money-grubby family members are squawking about it, but I know that my father wouldn't leave his important business to anyone but me.

I'm an only child, after all, and he's been training me to take over as Caputo since I was seventeen.

I walk around his desk, running my fingers along it. It's gotten dusty since I haven't allowed the cleaners to get in here since he passed.

Passed. That's what everyone kept saying. *"I'm so sorry to hear about your father's passing."* He didn't pass. He was murdered.

My phone rings.

"Hey, how are you holding?" Nico asks.

"Just going through his things." Nico is my best friend. I've known him for years. We are more like brothers than anything else. I know he'd give his life for me in a heartbeat and I'd do the same for him, even if it's his job to protect me and not the other way around.

"I just found my father's key ring on the desk, give me a sec," I say as I put him on speaker so I can unlock each of the drawers.

In the second to last drawer there's a stack of paper-work. "I've got something," I mention out loud to Nico.

"Anything useful?"

"Looks like his medical records, you know he had a bad ticker, right, even if it took a bullet to take him down."

"Yeah," he says grimly. "Fuckers. What else?"

"Stuff like my birth certificate, my mother's death certificate, things like that."

I remember when my mom died. "Of course they never solved my mom's murder. They won't be solving Dad's either. Cops are useless, unless you pay them, and even then they are a bunch of incompetent little bitches that can only whine and beg for more money."

Nico spits on the other side. "Pigs."

"Not like it matters, does it? Because at the end of the day, we both know who killed both my parents."

Luca Lorenzo. I'm almost certain of it.

"You know we own most of South Chicago, while Lorenzo rules over North Chicago. He doesn't like that he doesn't own the whole of Chicago, and he also doesn't like that he doesn't have a male heir."

"Just that girl you saved once, right?"

"Yeah. After that, Luca swears left and right that he doesn't have any beef with the Riccis. My dad might have believed him, but I know better than to believe Luca or anyone with the last name Lorenzo. Even if my father took strides to forgive Luca toward the end."

A memory assaults me. A fight we'd had in this very office.

"*You know he killed Mama!*" I burst out, *after we'd seen him at a party and my father had been friendly and charming toward him and his little daughter.*

"*We don't know that, Dante,*" *my father said with a sad little smile. "Your mother died because of me. Because I had my fingers in too many pies. It could have been anybody.*"

I gritted my teeth to keep from saying something disrespectful to my father. I loved him, and I'd always done what he said, but this? Luca Lorenzo?

"*We know he's our rival, and that he doesn't have an alibi for when she was killed,*" *I said tightly, and my father sighed.*

"*Don't you get tired, son? Of all the killing? Of always wanting revenge?*"

"*Never,*" *I said firmly, and my father ran a hand through his thick, mostly gray hair.*

"*What about that little daughter of his? What's her name? Mia? You saved her life a while back, you know that?*"

"*So what?*" *I asked, exasperated. "She's a little kid, I wasn't gonna let her get shot.*"

"*You took a bullet for Lorenzo's daughter, Dante. Of course he wants to make amends.*"

I scoffed. "It was just a scratch, and she could have been any kid."

"*Nevertheless, I think we need to accept this olive branch from Luca,*" *my father insisted. "So, no more scuffling around with his brothers and cousins, yeah?*"

I set my jaw but was silent.

"*Dante?*" *There was a warning tone in my father's voice, and I knew that I had no choice.*

"*Yes, Papa,*" *I said finally, and stalked out of his office.*

"Hey, man, you still there?" Nico's voice pulls me out of my head, but my rage toward Luca is still boiling.

"Yeah, I'm here."

I shuffle through the papers that I found in the locked drawer, and I come across my father's will, my heart jumping into my throat as I begin to read it.

"I found it," I near whisper it, but it's enough.

"Yeah? What does it say? Not that I have any question about it." Nico sounds eager. I know he is behind me and same as me, he is sure my dad wanted me to step up in his place.

Not surprisingly, he's left almost everything to me.

"Marisa got some of it, but yeah, we were right."

I don't mind that Marisa Lopez, our housekeeper, got a small amount in the will. She's a second mother to me. She's kind and lovely, and she deserves what my father left her. She was also his mistress for the last fifteen years.

"I'll go through this in detail and let you know if there are any surprises, But as far as I can see at first glance, it's pretty clear."

"Okay, let me know if you need anything."

We hang up and I read the whole thing with an eagle eye. No reason to just skim it only to have someone find something that will screw me over.

It's all pretty standard until I come across a section later in the will called A List of Wishes. It's probably not legally binding, but it lists out all of Papa's desires on how he wants to be cremated, how he wants the service, and then, at the bottom, he lists something that shocks me.

I wish for my son, Dante Ricci, to marry Mia Lorenzo.

What the hell? Mia is just a kid, for one thing, and she's Luca Lorenzo's daughter. I stare at it for a long while before the wheels in my head start turning.

What's the best way to get close to Luca Lorenzo? To punish him for what he did to my family?

Getting close to his daughter.

A smile spreads across my face as I take the will and slide it into a briefcase, taking it with me to the lawyer.

"Don't worry, Dante," Edgar Lent tells me, looking over the list of wishes. "This isn't legally binding, so you don't have to marry Mia Lorenzo."

I smile at him, showing my teeth. He looks a little nervous. I guess when we come to Edgar, usually something is terribly wrong, so he's worried that I might snap after my father's death.

Lucky for him, I'm pretty strong-willed, and I've got a plan that will help me grieve.

"But I want to marry her," I say, and Edgar blinks at me.

"What do you mean, you want to marry her?" he chokes out. "You're not the marrying type, Dante, how many times have you told me that?"

I shrug. "Well, I've changed my mind. I want to honor my father's wishes."

Edgar sputters. "Well, you'll have to have her consent, of course—"

"I'll get it," I say easily. "I'm meeting with Luca tonight."

"Tonight? You want this handled *tonight*?" Edgar shuffles through the will. "Dante, the estate can't be transferred to you right away—"

I wave a hand to dismiss him. "I don't care about that. I just want the wheels turning on my marriage."

Edgar just stares at me, looking shell-shocked.

"Well...okay. I'll handle all the paperwork when you get Miss Lorenzo's consent."

"Consider it done," I say, sliding him a stack of cash that he quickly slides into a drawer. As uptight as Edgar is, he always gets the job done, and I have no doubt that he'll have my father's estate transferred to me soon.

"You'll want a prenup, of course," he says, and I shake my head. Edgar blanches. "Dante, trust me. You *want* a prenup. With your assets, plus now, your father's estate—"

"I don't need a prenup," I say firmly, making my tone low and dangerous, and Edgar swallows hard.

"Fair enough," he mumbles, trying to put the papers all in one folder. He's nervous and trembling, and I understand, but I know what I am doing.

I stand up and clap a hand on his shoulder. "Don't be so nervous, Edgar. You'll get it done. I trust you."

"Yes," he says dumbly, and I walk out of the office to prepare for my meeting with Luca Lorenzo.

Mia Lorenzo is too young for me. I have a vague memory of the last time I saw her. She's not my type at all, too mousy, too flat, her legs too long. She was seventeen when I saved her from being caught in a crossfire, but four years won't have made much of a difference, I'm sure.

Not that it matters. She's just a means to an end, and that end will be Luca Lorenzo's life. I can't wait to hear him begging for his life as I aim the gun at the back of his head, the same way he did to my parents before pulling the trigger.

2

MIA

"Papa, I'm going out," I announce, sliding on my heels.

My father comes to the door of his office, frowning at me. "Not tonight, Mia," he says in a demanding voice that tells me I'm not going anywhere.

I deflate, finishing putting on my shoes, hoping against hope that something changes and I get to go out with my friends.

It's my best friend's birthday, and I really don't want to miss her party.

"Why not?" I ask and I know there's an edge to my voice. I don't ask for much, I really don't, and my father usually dotes on me, so I'm sure he has a very good reason for wanting to keep me home.

"Because we're having company for dinner," Papa says, gesturing for me to come into his office."

I do as he says and I sit down in the chair across from the desk, huffing out a breath.

"Why do you need me there for a business dinner?" I ask.

"Because Dante Ricci has requested your presence."

I sit straight up where I'd been slumping. "Dante? What could he want me there for?" I ask out loud, my heart beating too quickly in my chest.

"I don't know, Mia. But he saved your life, you know? Plus, he just lost his father. We owe him at least a dinner."

I nod, thinking that this might be better than any night out with my friends I could have imagined.

Dante Ricci is a *god* of a man, standing over a foot taller than my five-foot-two frame, broad shoulders, muscular back...these piercing hazel eyes and dark hair that he lets grow too long. I haven't seen him, other than just in passing at events, since I was seventeen.

I'd been just a kid, so of course I'd developed a crush on him. Who wouldn't? He'd been so brave, stepping in front of a bullet for me. I guess not much has changed in four years, given that my heart is doing backflips in my chest.

I can't wait to see Dante, and I smile at my father.

"I'll be there," I say, not wanting to appear too eager. But when I leave his office, I all but sprint upstairs to my room to change.

I don't want to wear a club dress when Dante's father has just died. They haven't had a service, yet, but all the mafioso will be invited, of course.

I'm glad that I'll get to see Dante before the ceremony, something less formal.

I change my dress about four times before settling on a sky-blue, low-cut number, not quite an evening gown but a little more than a cocktail dress. The blue looks good with my auburn hair, and it matches my eyes.

The cook is making veal chops for dinner and my mouth waters as she starts to cook them. I know I've put on a few pounds recently because I've been staying home too much, which is one of the reasons I was trying to get out of the house.

My dress fits a little tighter than expected and I keep pulling it down to cover more of my thick thighs, frowning.

Dante is half an hour late, and I'm a little annoyed but it's okay because Elena, our cook, has made us peppermint tea (she says it aids digestion) and I'm sipping it when our butler, Charles, announces, "Dante Ricci," and bows as Dante walks in the room. Dante smiles at Charles and all the air goes out of my lungs in a whoosh.

While I've been gaining weight the past four years, Dante has just been getting more attractive. There are a few lines around his eyes that just add to his rugged good looks, and there's stubble across his jaw, a little darker-colored than the hair on his head.

He's wearing an obviously tailored suit, and he takes off his jacket and sits it on his chair before sitting down, across from me. He looks right into my face and I freeze. I think this is the first time he's actually acknowledged me since the day he saved me.

"Hello, Mia. You're looking beautiful, as always," he says in a low, charming tone, and I can't help but smile at him.

"You look well, too, Dante." I pause. "I was so sorry to hear about your father. He was always kind to me."

I didn't know Dante's father that well, but Enzo had been kind to me on that day.

Suddenly, I'm no longer sitting at the dining table. I'm back there again. Back in the day where nearly everything changed for me.

I dropped to the ground, hiding under someone's desk. We were at a dinner party, and I didn't remember nor did I really care whose party it was. I'd never even seen a shootout, much less been involved in one, and my heart felt like it was going to climb out of my mouth.

I wasn't breathing well, hyperventilating and looking everywhere for my father.

"Hey, hold up!" a voice yelled from behind me and I whirled around to see Dante, holding his hands up. "You fucking idiots, there are children here!"

He walked toward the gunfire as I was trying to crawl away, kicking one of the shooter's legs out from under him.

I remembered thinking, even in my terrified haze, that he was awfully brave.

I turned slightly when the gunfire died down but the other guy kept shooting and bullets were whizzing by my head.

Dante ducked, crouching in front of me and grunting out when a bullet grazed his bicep.

"Are you okay, pretty girl?" he asked, and I looked up at him with wide eyes, terrified. I couldn't breathe. I couldn't do anything but stare at him as my heart seemed to seize up in my chest.

Dante put both his hands on my shoulders. "Breathe, kiddo. In through your nose, out through your mouth. Slow, yeah?"

I did as he said and I squeezed my eyes shut so I wouldn't see the blood trailing down his arm.

When I opened my eyes, Dante picked me up, bridal style, and carried me to my father, who took me from his arms and squeezed me tight.

"She'll be okay," Dante said, his voice tight with pain as he grimaced and looked at the wound on his arm.

"Dante, I can never repay you—"

"Forget it," Dante said harshly, leaving the room, and that was the last time I'd spoken to Dante Ricci.

I shake myself from the memory.

Later, I found out that it was just a stupid fight two cousins had over a girl, and it wasn't anything important to the mafioso at large. Luckily, no one was killed. I never did find out what punishment my father put on those boys, but I never saw them again, so I could assume it wasn't good.

"Thank you," Dante says easily, his smile fading. "You and your family are of course, invited to the service."

My father pipes up then. "When is the service, Dante?"

Dante shrugs. "Not sure yet. Waiting on the autopsy."

I hum in the back of my throat. I know that in our lifestyle, autopsies aren't performed very often. My heart goes out to Dante. I don't know how his dad died, but I can only assume it wasn't natural causes.

"Do you have any ideas about who did it?" my father asks, and Dante shoots him a look, something flashing in his hazel eyes.

"A couple. And the forensics from the autopsy will help clear any lingering doubts," he says, his voice low. "But let's not talk about such things at dinner." He smiles at me again, showing even, white teeth.

It's almost a predatory smile, and I'm not sure how to take it, so I clear my throat, blushing and looking down at my hands as Elena starts to serve the first course, some bone broth and fresh Italian bread.

Dante eats well, dipping his bread into the broth and praising Elena for her efforts, and she smiles at him brightly before heading back into the kitchen to finish up the main course.

"You've got quite a chef," Dante says, and my father smiles.

"She's been in the family for thirty years," he says.

Dante nods. "We have a housekeeper that's been with

us quite a while," he says. "She's taken to bed since Papa died."

My father sighs. "Surely you know that she was also his mistress?"

Dante raises an eyebrow. "Of course I did, but I'm surprised that you know."

My father chuckles. "I knew Enzo better than you think, son."

Dante stiffens just slightly at the way my father called him son, and I feel something tight starting in my throat.

During my life, I've had dinners with lots of dangerous men, some that even wanted to court me, but my father has always been protective, and he's kept me away from the *most* dangerous men.

Dante Ricci has a reputation, with women and with the law, having been arrested several times but getting off because of his excellent lawyer. Is Dante one of those dangerous men my father has been trying to keep me way from?

"What brings you to dinner tonight?" Papa asks, and Dante smiles, loosening up.

"A list of my father's last wishes in his will. There's one I need to discuss with you." Dante turns his gaze to me and I'm all but paralyzed by those hazel eyes of his. "And you, Mia."

"Me?" I put my napkin down in my lap, finishing chewing the bit of bread in my mouth.

"My father wants you to be my wife," he says, looking deeply into my eyes, and I choke even though there's nothing in my mouth.

3

DANTE

The look on Mia's face is priceless, and I can't help smirking. Luca, on the other hand, looks less shocked, almost like he's mulling it over.

"I suppose Enzo wanted our families to be closer," Luca murmurs.

Mia keeps choking on air, pressing the napkin to her mouth as she coughs, her pretty face turning red.

She's really grown up since the last time I'd seen her. In my head, she was still that seventeen year old scared little girl, but I guess that makes sense because it's been four years. Time goes by so quickly.

Mia is beautiful in a way that not many Italian girls are. She has bright blue eyes and red hair along with her straight nose and dimpled chin. She looks a lot like her mother, I suppose, although I've only seen the woman once or twice. Mia's mother is blonde and beautiful, but very Russian.

"What do you think, Mia?" I ask, leaning over the table toward her, wanting to get closer. I know I'm a nice looking guy and I'm hoping she is grateful enough I saved her life. I should be able to use that to get her to say yes, and then I'll find out more about how Luca killed my family. Once I have proof, Nico and the rest of my men will take care of it – unless I decide I want to take care of it myself.

"About...About getting m-married?" she stutters. "I don't even know you that well."

"Many marriages have started with less," Luca says, nodding as if he's made up his mind. "I think it's a good idea, Mia. Dante is a good man, and he'll take care of you."

Mia stares at her father, her mouth gaping open and shut like a fish. "Papa, I don't—"

"You don't want to marry me?" I ask, raising an eyebrow and smiling at her. "And here I thought you liked me," I tease.

Mia blushed an even brighter red. "Of course I like you," she mumbles. "But marriage is serious."

I hum. "And you're so young," I point out, and Mia frowns.

"I'm not *that* young," she complains.

"Then you're old enough to make your own decisions," I say, and she stares at me, something flashing in her blue eyes.

"Of course I am."

"So, what's your decision, Mia? Will you marry me?" I ask, leaning across the table to take her hand in my own, running my lips across her knuckles. She shivers, and that's when I know I've got her.

"Can I have some time to adjust to the idea before the wedding?" she asks meekly.

I shrug. "Of course. Whatever you want." I pause. "But I would like you to move in with me as soon as possible."

Mia's eyes widen and she looks at her father, who smiles and nods.

"It's time you left the nest, Mia," he says softly. "You've been so sheltered ever since the shootout."

I hum in agreement, even though I didn't know that she's been cooped up in the house basically since the shootout that I'd saved her from. I still have a bullet scar on my upper left bicep from it, but I'd do it all over again.

Not because I get to use her now but because she was only a kid.

She's got to be nearing twenty-one now, at least old enough to drink, old enough to marry, and since I'm only using her for one purpose, that's fine with me.

She stands up and pulls at her dress and I notice how thick her thighs are and my mouth goes dry.

Well... maybe two purposes. It wouldn't be so bad to bed her while I'm trying to get closer to her father, get the proof that I need.

Mia excuses herself from the table and Luca turns to me.

"This isn't just some scheme, is it?" he asks in an eerily calm voice.

I shake my head. "Absolutely not. My father wished for Mia and I to marry, and I want to obey his wishes. That's all."

"But you're not in love with my daughter."

"Love comes, does it not?" I ask, although I have no intention of falling in love. I don't even know if I can. I've never opened myself up enough to a woman, even after months-long flings. My life style doesn't bode well for life-long love. Love is a tool everyone else can use to hurt me with and I can't afford to let them.

"You're right," Luca murmurs. "My wife and I, we didn't know each other when she came from Russia," he admits.

I look at him as if fascinated, although I've heard this story before, from my father.

"I suppose it wasn't love at first sight," I muse, and Luca barks out a laugh.

"Absolutely not. She was terrified of me at first. But now..." He looks up at the family portrait of him, his wife, and Mia. "Now, she'd do anything for me and I'd die for her."

"That's a lovely story," I say, trying to keep the sarcasm out of my voice. I hate Luca Lorenzo, but I need to get as close to him as I can, to find out all his secrets. "Does that mean you'll give me your blessing to marry Mia?"

Luca looks at me for another long moment. "I don't think I have to tell you that if you hurt her..."

I wave a hand to dismiss him. "Yeah, you'll kill me. Got it," I say with a laugh, and Luca looks at me as if he's dead serious, and I know that he is.

He'd killed for less, and so had my father, to be honest.

Neither of them were honorable men, and neither am I. I'd never intentionally hurt a woman. I'm not a coward to prey on those who can't match me in every way. Besides, if all goes well, I intend to keep her happy enough until I reach my goal.

When she does end up getting hurt, it will be because I got my revenge, not because I acted against her or the institution of marriage in any way or form. Also, by then, her father won't be there to do anything about it.

"You have my blessing," Luca says finally, and I smile, standing up to shake his hand.

The main course, veal chops with butter penne, is delicious, and I finish my plate and look over at Luca.

"I think I'll take my future wife up a plate, if you don't mind," I say easily, and Luca nods.

"Anastasia will be down soon for dessert. She has a hell of a sweet tooth. You can meet her and have dessert with us before you go."

"Of course."

"Fourth door on the right," Luca tells me.

Elena wraps me up a plate of veal chops and pasta and I head up the stairs. I find the room easily enough. The door is closed, so I knock softly.

"Come in," Mia calls, and I open the door to find her in just her slip, brushing her long, auburn hair.

She squeaks, covering herself. "Dante! I wasn't expecting you."

"You missed the main course," I murmur, looking her in the face instead of at her body, even though it's a struggle.

I place the plate in front of her, crossing my arms and leaning against her wall.

"Are you nervous around me, Mia?" I ask her, smiling, and she flushes again but keeps eye contact with me.

"Yes," she says simply. "You are a bit intimidating. And you're in my room. I haven't had any men besides my father in my room."

I grin. "That's good news to me."

She finally cracks a little smile. "Why, because you want me all to yourself?"

"Isn't that what every man wants from his wife?"

Mia swallows visibly. "Do you really want me to be your wife?"

I simply nod.

"Why? Just because it's what your father wanted?" she asks, and I'm taken aback. I stand up straight.

"No," I defend myself. "But I won't deny that has a lot to do with it. I never saw myself getting married." I pause, looking for a reaction from her but her face remains blank. "But when I thought about it, you're the right choice."

"What makes me the right choice? Because it would unite our families?"

"That's one of the reasons," I say, trying to quickly think of something else. If she says no to this marriage, my plans will be ruined. "But also, you're a very beautiful woman, Mia."

She bites her lip. "But I only want to marry for love, Dante. Could you love me?"

"In time, I know I could," I say, taking her hand and kissing it. She's almost all but agreed, and I think maybe she needs just a tip over the edge, so I straighten up and then lean down to kiss her, brushing my lips against hers chastely.

Mia makes a surprised sound against my mouth, and then she sticks her tongue between my parted lips, shocking me.

I kiss her deeply, searching her mouth with my tongue and putting my arms around her waist to pull her closer.

She tastes like mint and some rich chocolate that she must have snuck after dinner. My heart is thudding too hard against my chest plate. I have the feeling that she's inexperienced due to her age, but she doesn't kiss like it. Kissing Mia Lorenzo is a lot hotter than I expected, and I chase her lips with my own when she finally pulls away so that she can breathe.

Then she smiles.

"Okay. I'll move in next week," she says.

I'm breathing hard as she ushers me out of her room and closes the door.

What have I gotten myself into?

4

MIA

Four days later, my father's men are moving all of my things into Dante's mansion, and I stand in the foyer, watching them.

I'm still thinking about Dante, how he brought me dinner after I'd excused myself early. It surely means he's interested, right? And maybe this isn't just because of his father's wishes? The way he'd kissed me...

I have to think that he really wants this, or else I'll never go through with it.

"Are you sure all this furniture is okay?" I ask as they take the wraparound red leather couch I'd had set up in my huge room upstairs.

"Of course," Dante says absent-mindedly. He's on his phone; I assume for business. My father sure is attached to his, and they're in the same line of business. "Place needs a woman's touch."

"I like the red," Marisa says. Dante's already introduced me to his housekeeper, and she looks pale and drawn, with bags under her eyes.

"Father's service will be on Saturday," Dante says,

looking up at Marisa instead of at me. "That sound good, Marisa?"

She nods before covering her face with her hands and running upstairs.

"She's taking it really hard," I comment.

"That's because they were lovers," Dante says bluntly, and I blink at him.

"Your father had a mistress?"

"Not while Mama was alive, but after, yes."

"Do you believe in having mistresses while you're married?" I ask, my tone sounding accusatory. I know that a lot of men in the famiglia have wives and mistresses, but that isn't something that I want to put up with.

"Of course not," Dante says, frowning as if he finds it offensive, but I swear he's hiding a smirk.

"Better not," I mumble, and Dante laughs, coming down the stairs to sweep me up into his arms.

I giggle, not used to this kind of affection from him (or anyone, really, my father kept me well protected), but I love it. He kisses along the side of my face. I'm nervous to spend the night here, since we haven't done anything other than kiss, and that was just once in my bedroom that first night.

And I haven't been with a man since I was in high school, so there's that.

I'm not exactly a virgin but I'm certainly not experienced, and I have an idea that Dante *is*. I've heard about his reputation, how he brings home a girl every week.

Dante puts me down and kisses the back of my neck, making me shiver.

"I need to go out for a bit. Feel free to snoop around, pretty girl," he says in a low voice, right next to my ear, and I shiver again.

Dante exits the house without telling me where he's going, but I'm definitely used to that with my father.

I guide the guys to bring in the rest of my stuff, most of it going up to the master bedroom, and then I walk upstairs, touring the house. It's a mansion about the size of my father's, something like ten or twelve bedrooms, a huge kitchen, an infinity pool in a heated pool house out back. I can't wait to go into the pool. We have one, but my father never liked the idea of heating it.

The only door that's locked upstairs is at the end of the hall, and I frown, trying to look through the keyhole. All I can see is a desk, and I assume it must be Dante's office, or maybe his father's. That's probably why it's locked.

I walk into my room and open one of my suitcases and pull out my bikini, changing into it.

The infinity pool is warm and feels amazing, and when I duck my head under I realize it must be a saltwater pool.

I do a few laps, losing track of time and floating around, until I hear a voice, echoing through the pool house.

"You like it?"

I start to tread water, looking up to see Dante standing at the end of the infinity pool, unbuttoning the cuffs of his shirt. He's already thrown his suit jacket onto a lounge chair.

"You're getting in with me?" I ask, excited but nervous. I guess Dante's expecting me to act as his wife immediately, but if he doesn't think he'll have to woo me, he's got another thing coming.

Dante smiles, showing his teeth.

I can't get the measure of that smile. It's not his half-smile, showing a dimple in one cheek, one that's charming. That toothy smile seems like one a crocodile would give to his prey, and I'm not sure what to think of it.

"I don't have my swimsuit on, so I'm skinny dipping," he says, before taking off his shirt and dropping his hands to his waistband.

I look away, blushing, but then I figure: this is going to be my husband, right? So, I wade over to the shallow end of the pool and untie my bikini top and bottoms, throwing them up onto the edge of the pool.

Dante grins again, this time one of those charming ones, and dives into the water, stark naked. I don't have time to stare at all the expanse of bronze skin he's displaying before he swims up to me, tickling my feet.

I kick and giggle and he comes up out of the water, splashing me and rubbing a hand across his face.

"Hi, there," he murmurs, sliding his hands around my waist and standing up. We're still in the shallow end. His hands move across my ass and I gasp, arching my back. I wrap my arms around his neck, wanting more, my body aching.

He grabs two handfuls of my ass this time, lifting me up and pressing his erection against my core, and I cry out, burying my face in his neck.

"Kiss me there," he demands, and I do as he says, kissing him open-mouthed, even nipping slightly at the skin.

Dante groans and moves me to the edge of the pool, putting me up there while I whine.

He tsks. "Don't worry, pretty girl. I'm going to take care of you."

I've barely spent any time with this man, but he's going to be my husband, and I've wanted him for a long time.

I bite my lip as I look down at him, and then he buries his face in my sex, pressing his lips to my clit while he slides a finger inside of me.

It's tight at first but I become slick and hot easily as he

suckles my clitoris, pressing his finger deeper and eventually adding another.

He hooks his fingers up and I moan loudly. Dante hums, moving his mouth to my inner thigh.

"That's it, baby. Be loud for me."

Then he locks his lips around my clit again and pumps his fingers in and out of me, faster and faster until I'm arching my back, crying out his name, my thighs trembling around his head.

When I come, black spots appear across my vision, and I gasp in breath like I've been drowning.

Dante moans and slowly removes his fingers as I continue to shudder. He hefts himself out of the pool, naked, and now I can see how tight his abdomen is, how broad his chest. He has a tattoo on his left pec, a snake that winds around toward his nipple.

He's also a lot bigger than the guy I was with in high school, and for a moment, I wonder if he'll fit. I bite my lip, looking up into his eyes and his hazel eyes change from lust-filled to concerned.

"Are you okay, pretty girl?" he asks, and that's all I need. I smile brightly at him and spread my thighs forward as he covers my body with his own.

"I'm perfect, Dante," I say honestly, and he guides himself into me, pushing in slowly to get me used to his girth and length. He's gritting his teeth, holding back, and I gasp, rocking my hips to try to make it better.

After a long moment, he starts to slide forward and backward, and I'm so slick from my previous orgasm that the slide becomes easy after just a couple of strokes. It begins to feel good again instead of just uncomfortable, and I brace my hands on his shoulders for purchase. His mouth parts as he pumps in and out of me, his hazel eyes dark and half-lidded, darting from my face to my breasts and then back again as he looks into my eyes.

"Feels so good," I murmur, feeling lightheaded from all the excitement and his nearness.

He smells like saltwater and sandalwood and sin, the cross chain he wears around his neck bouncing in my face.

"You feel like hot velvet," Dante grunts, and as he begins to even out his strokes, I feel the orgasm building in my lower abdomen again.

I've never come twice in such short succession, and it feels amazing when I shudder and clench around him.

Dante groans loudly. I never knew a man could be this vocal during sex, and I love it. I love the way I know my body is making him feel good.

He spills inside of me after just a few more strokes and I let out a long breath, kissing along the side of his face.

Dante kisses me back, on the lips, but it's brief and chaste before he pulls out of me, going to the lawn chair to grab me a towel.

I frown as I wrap it around myself. "Where are you going?"

"I've got some work to deal with," he says breathlessly, rubbing a towel over himself, still nude and unashamed.

I frown deeper. "Didn't you just leave to do some work."

"It never ends, Mia," he says in a teasing tone, and leans down to kiss me once more before heading back to the other end of the pool house to put his clothes back on.

I watch him dress, trying not to be disappointed. I know that men like Dante and my father are busy, and I know that what they do is important, but I want more of Dante. Especially in this getting-to-know-each-other stage.

"We haven't even been out on a real date," I say.

"I'll make you dinner tonight," he promises.

"You can cook?" I ask incredulously. I'm not judging, because I sure can't.

Dante chuckles. "My mother taught me how to make the world's best ziti. You'll see. I'll see you in a couple of hours."

I watch him leave, wondering just where he's going and what he's doing.

I know from being my father's daughter that the work part of Dante's life would remain a secret to me, but I can't help feeling nervous. Dante's reputation as a womanizer is beginning to really set in, and I need to know he's not being unfaithful.

But he's given me full rein to snoop through his house, and surely if he was seeing someone, he wouldn't do that.

Maybe I just need to learn to trust my new fiancé.

5

___

DANTE

I'm not exactly lying to my new fiancée. I *do* have work to do, even if it's the kind of work that I enjoy. I've been invited to a party, and I have to turn down a few women there and make the announcement that I'm engaged to Mia.

I have plenty of a reputation, and although Luca didn't seem too concerned with it, I know that Mia is. I can't have her calling this off before I get closer to Luca and the secrets of her family.

I don't hold the same animosity toward Mia as I do Luca. After all, she probably has no idea what her father gets up to. That's how it is in our world. Our wives and daughters, even mistresses, don't know what we do other than a cursory idea. We keep it from the women, because it's dangerous work, and no one wants them hurt. It's unethical as a wise guy to even hurt women and children, even in a dire situation.

I have no intention of hurting Mia – but I can't say the same for her father. Mia's a fun time, with her tight little body and her pretty face, and part of getting closer to her is getting intimate with her. She seems to love it as much as I do, and I definitely can use the stress relief.

It doesn't mean anything to me, even if it means something to her. I can't let it mean anything and I feel a little bad about that, how she clearly has feelings for me when I don't have any for her. I never will. But that's kind of been the story of my life.

Speaking of that story, Doreen Rossi walks up to me at the party. Doreen is one of the women I've hook up with on occasion.

"Dante," she croons, putting her hand on my upper arm. "You look well."

I slowly move away from her, smiling. "You look great as usual, Doreen."

She pouts, noticing my different demeanor. "What's going on with you? You're not acting like yourself."

I usually wouldn't mind her coming on to me, but today, I'm on a mission to make everyone believe my womanizing days are over. And I suppose in a way, they are, at least for a while. I don't plan on giving Mia any reason to doubt me.

I need her to be in love with me so that I can get closer to her...and closer to Luca. She needs to think that I'm serious, and that we're family.

"Things have changed," I admit, and Nico walks up to me, looking at me with that intense stare of his.

"What have you done?" he asks in a low tone, and I know that he's heard.

I grin. "I got engaged," I announce, and Doreen stares at me blankly.

"You're lying," she says flatly.

"Why would I lie? My father wished for me to get married to Mia Lorenzo, and so I'm giving him his final wish."

"Why would he want you to marry a Lorenzo, of all people?" Nico asks, while Doreen excuses herself to the bar.

I shrug, although I have an idea that my father wanted me to know the truth about Luca, too. There's no other reason he could have wanted me to marry Mia.

Nico looks at me coolly, and I know that he'll want more information, but I'm not even letting my best friend in on this.

For all he knows, I'm happily engaged.

"You don't love her," Doreen states, out of nowhere, when I walk up to the bar where she's standing. She's throwing back martinis.

"Not yet," I admit. "But love comes, they say."

Doreen scoffs. "You're throwing your life away on that prude."

I raise an eyebrow. "She hasn't been a prude with me," I comment, slightly annoyed that Doreen is talking about Mia that way. And after that, she shuts her mouth.

Mia may be young, but I wouldn't describe her as a prude. Delicious, yes. Innocent, also yes. Prude, no way.

I grab my drink and walk back into the foyer, mingling.

Luca Lorenzo shows up after an hour or so, and I'm only on my second drink, nursing it. I want all my wits about me.

He says hello to me and pulls me into a hug.

"Has Dante told everyone he's going to be my son?" he announces, and my blood runs cold at his words. I'll *never* be his son. I grit my teeth, telling myself that this is the only way to take him down.

"I've been telling everyone," I say, giving him a tight smile. "Mia's a little worried about my reputation, so I wanted everyone to know."

Luca laughs. "We all have reputations when we're young and unmarried," he says dismissively.

I don't mention that he had some overlap between his Russian wife and his mistresses.

Nico is on his way to drunk, which is unusual for him, but it is his day off and he is here as a guest too, so I just take a few videos and laugh.

"Why didn't you bring her?" Luca asks.

"We're still getting settled in," I respond. I will eventually start bringing Mia to some of these events, especially parties like this, because I want us seen together plenty, but she doesn't need to witness all the women throwing themselves at me on day one, before I have the chance to warn them off. They know I'm not a relationship kind of guy, or wasn't at least, so they tend to show no respect if I'm with someone.

And I wanted them to also have the curtesy of knowing I'm no longer available without rubbing it in or making it look like Mia is just another woman on the rotation. Because she's not.

Luca nods, heading to the bar to get himself a drink.

Felicia Nunez is the next woman to walk up to me, and like Doreen, I've hooked up with her quite a few times. We've been on and off again with a physical relationship for years. She knows it will never be more than that, though. No feelings involved ever.

"I hear you're getting married," she says, her face slightly hurt, and I give her a sympathetic smile.

"It was bound to happen, Felicia," I say gently.

She shakes her head, cracking a smile. "I guess I thought it never would."

Felicia is fun to be around, but it was never more than that. Still, I understand this is the end of our history together. She is on the list of women I need to break it off with after agreeing to marry Mia, so I'm glad it's done.

"You're going to be a faithful husband," Luca says, sitting at the bar, having heard the conversation between me and Felicia.

"And a loyal son," I say, although it feels like poison in my mouth.

Luca looks over at me curiously. "You want to be involved in the family business?"

I shrug. "I think that's what Papa must have wanted. For us to merge our ideas and our men."

Luca nods, looking at me with a smile. "Enzo was a smart man."

I just sip my drink, looking at my watch. It's been a little over two hours since I left Mia back at the pool.

"I need to go home to my future wife," I say, and Luca claps me on the shoulder.

"You're a good man, Dante."

I want to laugh. I'm using his daughter and I have designs to kill him. So, "good" is not the best word to describe me.

I make my way through the party, saying my goodbyes, and finally get out of there, sighing as I sit at the steering wheel in my sports car.

I'm already socially exhausted, and I have to keep this personality "on" tonight, too, with Mia. It's going to be like I'm playing a part for months, possibly a year or two, before I can get what I want.

I make it back home and Mia's sitting in the living room, looking bored, her head hanging off the couch.

"You're home!" she exclaims, sitting up too fast and swaying.

I can't help but chuckle at her. "I've got everything for ziti in the kitchen. You want to help?"

"Okay," she says hesitantly. "But I'm no good at even boiling water."

"I don't know if I believe that," I murmur, but I honestly do. Mia may not be as spoiled as some of the famiglia princesses that I've met, but her father takes care of her.

I put her on chopping the onions and tears are streaming unbidden down her face by the time she's done.

I handle the garlic and then wash my hands, chuckling and wiping her tears away.

"Didn't mean to make you cry," I tease, and Mia sniffles, laughing.

"Elena has a trick but I don't know what it is," she complains.

"Well, it's all done now, just need to wait on the sauce." I put all the vegetables in to simmer and finish up the sauce before leading Mia out of the kitchen to the foyer.

"What do we do while we wait?" she asks, smirking up at me.

"I can think of a couple things," I say in a low tone, but Mia gets down on the floor and crawls toward where I'm standing, putting her hands on my belt buckle.

I look down at her with lust-filled eyes and think maybe being married isn't so bad after all.

6

MIA

I've lost my nerves since Dante and I made love for the first time, and I'm ready for more, so I lick my lips and unbuckle his slacks, tugging them down over his ass along with his boxer briefs.

"Maybe you can't cook, but you're great in other ways," Dante teases, putting his hand in my long hair.

I look up at him with a grin and lick a stripe up his plumping cock, right along a vein there. Dante groans, biting his lip as I take him into my mouth.

I'm slow and just enjoy the taste of him on my tongue, how heavy he feels in my mouth. I make sure there's plenty of saliva to lubricate him, and cover my teeth as he starts to thrust in my mouth.

I should have known: Dante isn't the type of man to let a woman take control. He ends up fucking my throat, my eyes watering as I gag a couple of times, his hand fisted loosely in my hair. He doesn't tug, just rolls his hips into my mouth.

I think I might have to tap out after a few moments, but

then Dante freezes, his hips stuttering as he spills into my mouth.

I gasp in air as he pulls out of me and Dante's face is instantly concerned.

"Fuck, I didn't hurt you, did I?"

"Of course not," I say hoarsely. "I wanted to make you feel good."

"You succeeded," he says with a laugh, kissing my forehead.

He adjusts himself back into his pants and goes to check the food and I'm hot between my legs and aching, wishing that we had time for more.

Surely, there would be more tonight.

Dante sets the table and we sit at one end of the huge table. His ziti is indeed, amazing, and I moan when I take a bite.

"I take it that means you like it?" he asks, and I nod eagerly.

"I love a man that can cook," I admit, and it's true, especially since I can't do it myself. "But don't you have a cook?"

Dante shakes his head. "No, not really. Marisa used to cook for Papa, but since he passed, she hasn't really felt like it."

"Oh, I'm sorry," I say, looking at him sympathetically.

Dante's face goes blank just for a second before he smiles back at me. I tilt my head, looking at him. There's something just under the surface with Dante. He puts on a brave face, acts as if he's taking his father's death in stride, but I can sense the pain behind his eyes.

"It's okay. I don't mind cooking," Dante says easily, and I clear my throat.

"Your father's service," I start. "You want me to come, right?"

Dante looks at me. "Of course I do. You're going to be my wife, and it was Father's wishes that we marry."

I swallow some ziti too hard and cough, sipping my chilled white wine.

I keep coming back to that. How it was his father's wish that he marry me and not exactly his idea.

"Besides," Dante says, as if he can hear my thoughts, "I want you there."

"Of course, I'll be there," I say. "My father extends his respect, as well."

"I've invited Luca," Dante says tightly, spearing some more ziti, and I sense something there, too, between my father and him.

It's probably work related, and I know nothing about that.

I mean, of course, I know that my father and Dante are both famiglia, that they don't exactly operate inside of the law, but as to the specifics...I'm in the dark, and I don't mind staying that way.

When we finish dinner, Dante clears the dishes, taking them to the kitchen and leaving them there for the housekeeper.

"You've got your own bedroom for the time being," Dante says suddenly, and I blink at him.

"What do you mean, my own bedroom?" I ask. I've already moved all my things into the master bedroom.

"I just thought maybe you'd be more comfortable..." he starts. "At least until we tie the knot."

I snicker. "I'm clearly not that traditional, Dante."

Dante's smile seems a little off. "Fair enough. We'll share a bed, then."

I head upstairs, waiting for him to follow, and after finishing his wine, he does.

He undresses down to his boxer briefs and slides into bed, and I do the same, but nude.

"You sleep naked?" he murmurs, running his hands over my hips and ass.

"Always," I say easily.

Dante licks his lips. "I don't know how I'm going to get any sleep like this."

I cock my head, looking at him. "Dante, have you ever had a serious girlfriend? Someone that you lived with?"

He slowly shakes his head. "I haven't."

"So, you're not used to sleeping next to someone," I point out.

Dante grins sheepishly, ducking his head and hiding it in my neck. "You caught me."

"If you're uncomfortable, we could start off in different rooms," I suggest, hoping that he says no, and thankfully Dante shakes his head.

Relief washes over me. I know that I'm sort of a clingy person, but sleeping in the same bed together is so intimate and it's something I want to share with my husband.

I started out hoping that we would be intimate again tonight, but since Dante isn't used to having a woman in his bed, I just turn around and cuddle back up against him.

He's half hard beneath my ass but I ignore it, turning to kiss him goodnight.

"You're gonna get used to having me here," I murmur, and Dante kisses along my hairline, the back of my neck, like he did earlier today.

I drift off feeling happy and secure.

The next morning, Dante's hard-on is a lot more insistent and he groans against my neck, kissing me there and nipping at the skin.

"Good morning," I say with a stretch, just wiggling back against him further, and Dante bites down on my shoulder so hard it makes me gasp.

"You're doing this on purpose," he accuses, his voice hoarse from sleep. "You've been rubbing that ass all over me for an hour."

I giggle. "And you just waited for me to wake up? What a gentleman."

"Of course I did," he says almost defensively. "I only like willing participants."

"I'd be willing if I was asleep," I answer, and Dante barks out a laugh. I hear him shift, pushing down his underwear, and then he lifts one of my legs, sliding smoothly inside me.

I cry out and then hide my face in the pillow.

"Ah ah," Dante scolds, tugging on my hair. "What did I say about letting me hear you?"

"Fuck," I curse, as Dante starts to move inside me.

I thought I'd be nervous again, sleeping in Dante's bed. I thought that maybe he'd get up and leave since he wasn't used to sleeping with someone, but I'm so glad that he didn't.

"Fuck," Dante agrees. "You're so tight, pretty girl."

He starts to fuck me harder and I grab onto the headboard with one hand, pushing back against him to get him deeper. He fills me up so completely that it always starts out *almost* uncomfortable, but then quickly turns to pleasure that I've only been able to imagine before now.

"I'm not going to last," he warns, and I whimper.

"Me either." I'm quickly vaulting to my orgasm and it hits me like a train, making my head feel light and dizzy.

Dante growls as he comes inside of me, biting down on my shoulder again.

I run my hand along the bite. "That's going to leave a mark."

"Good," he murmurs. "Want everyone to know you're mine."

Heat floods through my body. Whatever worries I'd had about Dante and his "reputation" are fading away quickly.

I'm getting married to Dante Ricci, and I'm happy.

7

DANTE

My father's service comes too quickly. It's Saturday before I know it, and Mia is getting dressed in a black dress that trails all the way to her ankles. It's modest but still looks beautiful on her. I'm wearing my best black suit and my father's cufflinks.

I've been sleeping next to Mia for the better part of a week now, and yet I still haven't gotten to know her any better. Mostly, because I can't keep my damn hands off her.

We usually end up making love immediately, and then maybe having a bit of pillow talk. I've used her body and her strength to get through this week before my father's service, I have to admit.

I feel almost bad about it. Almost.

Mia finishes dressing before I do, her auburn hair plaited down her back, and she walks downstairs.

"Which car are we taking?" she asks.

"Nico is picking us up," I call downstairs, following her down.

When we get in the limousine, she puts her hand high

up on my thigh and I cover it with my own hand, squeezing hers lightly.

She smiles up at me and squeezes back.

"It's going to be a beautiful service, Dante."

My father wanted to be cremated, so we won't be having an open casket, just a gold-plated coffin filled with his ashes. I'm supposed to give the eulogy, but I'm not sure I can without breaking down.

"I don't know if I can do this," I say in a hushed whisper.

Mia leans her head against my shoulder.

"You'll do fine, Dante. I know how much you loved and respected your father."

Tears catch in my throat. Mia knows the right thing to say, almost all the time, and I've been maybe a little wary of getting closer to her. I can't imagine falling for her, but at the same time, isn't that what happens? When you let women in?

I wouldn't know. I've never done it.

So, I don't talk about my father. I don't talk about anything serious, regaling Mia with some stories from my youth, how I'd gotten arrested, the crew I hung around with. All funny, exciting stories. Nothing serious.

She'd trailed her hand along the knife scar on my back a couple of nights ago.

"How did you get this?" she asked, and I chuckled, shaking my head.

"A story for another time," I lied, not planning on ever telling her that story.

Our wedding will be in another week. I talked it over with Mia, how I don't want to wait too long. By then I'm hoping to be closer to her, closer to Luca.

Mia had been a bit reticent at first, worried we didn't

know each other enough, but given that we have my father's service, she eventually accepted. She thinks she is as close to ready as she'll ever be and I know she wants something happy to take our minds off these times, I suppose. Plus, we've been spending so much time together that I think I've gotten her to trust me, at least a bit.

When we arrive at the cemetery, we walk up toward the casket, which is already closed.

Nico parks and follows us there. Marisa is already there, crying into a handkerchief that had belonged to my father.

Mia stands next to me as we wait for everyone to arrive. Everyone shows up pretty quickly, and there's a lot of us. There's plenty of Riccis, including family and friends. But there is also Mia's parents, and a few representatives of the other famiglias, the Gallos, the Barones, the Espositos. Most of our men are also here paying their respects.

This is a day of peace between famiglias. A day to show our respect for a man who lived and died for his family.

And I'm glad that we're having the ceremony outside, because Papa wouldn't have wanted it in a church.

He and Mama hadn't married in a church, and although he was what you might call a lapsed Catholic, we never went to Mass.

Luckily, I'd greased a few palms and was getting his ashes buried in the Catholic cemetery.

Marisa made the sign of the cross and both my uncle Roberto and my cousin Leo went up to say a few words. I look over at Marisa, who's all broken up, and make my way through the crowd to her.

I lean down to speak to her. "You should say something," I say hoarsely, tears caught in my throat.

She shakes her head, looking up at me with watery green eyes. "I can't, Dante. *You* have to."

I take in a shaky breath and Mia pats me on the shoulder, having followed me over. I swallow down more tears, thinking I'm going to be nauseous after a while of this, and head up to the microphone that the priest has set up.

"My father was a hard-working man," I start. "But that's not why we're all here today. We're here to celebrate his life, just like he'd want. He wouldn't want us all to mope around."

The crowd tittered through their sobs.

"He was a fun-loving guy," I continued with a shaky smile. "He wouldn't want all of you crying. He loved my mother, he loved me, and he loved all of you in one way or another," I say, looking directly at Marisa. Maybe my father had never married her, but she was part of the family nonetheless. "But more importantly, Enzo loved life, and we should all celebrate that. So, I invite you all to come to a wake at Denny's bar."

"What are we, Irish?" my uncle Roberto groans, but he's joking and I smile at him.

Denny, the owner of the bar in question, steps up. "First round free for everyone here," he says, and for some reason, that's when I break down crying.

I guess because it's over. I guess because I've done all I can do and it is what my father would want, a celebration. A party.

I cover my face with my hands, crying, and Mia comes to me, taking me in her arms and sitting me down away from all the people.

"It's okay to be upset, Dante. He's your father," she says, and I take in a shaky breath, trying to hold back the tears.

I wipe at my face. "I'm okay," I say.

"You're not," she says, looking at me pointedly. "But that's okay. We're going to get through this."

I lean against her, taking more of her strength, and a spear of guilt spreads through me.

The guilt is gone by the time I throw back a fourth beer at Denny's, though, and Mia is drinking her fruity rum runners right along with me. Uncle Roberto sings one of my father's favorite Italian operas in a truly horrific accent, having forgotten much of the Italian he was taught as a kid, and we all laugh at him.

It's a party, all right, and by the end of it, I'm well and truly drunk, and even Mia is stumbling in her heels.

Nico's stayed veritably sober and he drives us home as I fight tears again, the alcohol hanging over me in a haze.

My father's gone. He'll never have a party like this again, and it's Luca Lorenzo's fault.

I manage to keep it back, though, and it's helped by Mia being there, by her taking my hand.

"If you want to be alone tonight," she says softly, but I shake my head, taking her into my arms when we enter the mansion.

She helps me upstairs and all but undresses me, and I whine, pulling her into the bed before she can get her dress unzipped.

Mia laughs and manages to wiggle out of her dress, but this time, I'm not interested in her body. This time, I'm only interested in her warmth, her murmured words of comfort.

I sleep next to her, and for the first time in my life, let a woman that isn't my mother comfort me. I suppose I need it, after losing my father and making a plan to avenge him.

I haven't had time to grieve, and Mia is letting me do that.

It might be more difficult than I thought not to let her in.

8

MIA

It already feels like I'm married to Dante by the time Saturday, the day before the wedding, rolls around. We've spent every minute together that he isn't working, and I'm happy as a clam.

Until, that is, I hear Dante in his office, speaking lowly into the phone.

"I'm not that kind of guy anymore," he says in a murmur, and then he chuckles low in his throat. "And of course I remember."

I frown, getting closer to the office door, and I swear I can hear a woman's voice on the line.

"No, of course not. I barely remember the day of the shootout," he says, and my heart drops to my feet.

Dante saved my life. It's a crucial moment in my life, one that I come back to all the time when I feel unsure about Dante's love, when I feel unsure about this marriage.

Who is he talking to?

Dante gets closer to the door, shutting it, and my heart flips over in my chest, anxiety rushing over me.

I head back to my room, all kind of awful thoughts swirling in my head.

Is he already having an affair? Before we even officially get married?

He'd given me his mother's ring, for God's sake. I look at it, frowning. Surely, he's just talking about work.

But why would he bring up the shootout?

While I'm trying to get through my emotions, Dante knocks on the door.

"Mia?"

"We're not supposed to see each other before the wedding," I call in a strained voice.

Dante pauses and then tries the door. I've locked it.

"Mia, come on. You're the one who said you weren't traditional."

"I'm traditional about this!" I insist, and Dante chuckles.

"All right, fair enough. I'm going out for a few hours."

Going out. Of course he was.

"I'm staying at my friend Marta's for the night," I call back.

Dante pauses again. "What?"

"Tradition," I remind him, and Dante groans.

"All right, whatever you want, pretty girl," he says, and I hear him going down the stairs.

I hadn't made those plans with Marta, because I really am not the traditional type, but now, I feel like I need some time away from Dante to sort out how I feel.

If he *is* having an affair, I need to know about it.

I call Marta. "Be ready in ten minutes," I say.

"Ready for what?" she asks.

"A stakeout," I say firmly.

"I'm not crazy," I say to my best friend as she stares at me in awe.

"You're not crazy. You're just following your fiancé on the day before your wedding because...you heard him talking on the phone?"

"It was *weird*, Marta! It was...flirty," I insist, huffing out a breath.

Marta rolls her eyes. "Sure. Not crazy at all."

"I just want to put my mind at ease," I say.

My best friend shifts in the passenger side of my car.

"I don't know, Mia. This could get dangerous, given what Dante does....."

Marta knows the score. She comes from a member of the famiglia just like I do, and neither of us sticks our noses in our family business.

"It's not about business," I say quickly. "I don't care about that. I just want to make sure he isn't cheating."

"I don't understand how you can think that just from one phone conversation..." she trails off when I don't answer, parked outside the gate of the mansion that Dante's car had pulled into. There are other cars on the street, so it doesn't look too obvious.

"We've been sitting here for hours," Marta complains. "Can't we at least leave to get food?"

"We'll get lunch later," I say, staring at the mansion, hoping (or not hoping) to see a woman coming out of there.

Dante finally comes out alone, and I let out a long breath.

He drives away, seemingly not noticing my car, and heads down the street. I throw the car into gear and follow him while Marta gasps and grabs on to the car door for purchase.

"You drive like a bat out of hell on the best of days," she grumbles, but I ignore her.

When Dante pulls into a hotel, my heart drops to my toes.

"*Bastardo*," I mutter.

"It doesn't mean anything," Marta says as I drive by the hotel, knowing that he'll see my car in the parking lot. She puts a hand on my knee. "It doesn't have to mean anything. Our family does a lot of in and out business in hotels."

I know that she's right, but I can't help suspecting.

I don't know how to ask him about it without revealing that I was eavesdropping, but I feel nauseous at the thought of it.

I haven't responded to Marta and she squeezes my knee.

"Are you still going to marry him?"

I swallow hard, thinking of Dante's hazel eyes, how he smiles at me after we make love, how he cried in my arms at his father's service.

"Do you think you can grow to love someone?" I ask Marta.

"Yes," she says hesitantly. "I do."

"Then I'll still marry him," I say. "But I'm going to have a conversation with him after the wedding, and tell him that I won't put up with cheating."

"There's no evidence he is cheating," Marta says, sounding exasperated.

"There's no evidence he isn't," I insist, and she groans.

"I think this wedding is making you crazy," she says, and I sigh, rubbing a hand over my face as we approach Marta's apartment complex.

She's moved out of the family home with a couple of

college roommates who are currently at home on spring break.

"Thank you for letting me stay tonight," I say, looking at her gratefully.

"What are best friends for?" she responds easily, and when we get inside her apartment, she instantly starts making me a rum runner.

"You're the best friend in the world," I groan, sipping it when she hands it to me.

"If I didn't get you drunk before your wedding, I'd be a terrible friend. Especially since you wouldn't let me throw you a bachelorette party."

I glower. "Mostly because I didn't want Dante to have a bachelor party."

"You're not the jealous type at all," she drawls.

I spend the rest of the night drinking rum runners and talking to Marta, and by the time I lie down on her couch, Dante has texted me a few times.

Miss you, pretty girl.

Can't wait for tomorrow.

I groan, my head aching as I roll over on Marta's couch.

I miss you, too, I text back, because I'm drunk and it's true. I misspell a couple of words since I'm squinting at my phone with one eye, and I nearly drop my phone in shock when Dante calls me.

"Hello?" I answer, my voice hoarse from drinking.

"Are you drunk?" he asks me, a smile in his voice.

"Maybe a little," I admit. "Marta said she didn't get to throw me a bachelorette party."

Dante hums. "Fair enough. No strippers, though, right?"

"None of your business," I tease, but Dante goes silent on the other line. "No, of course no strippers."

"Good. I didn't book any either," he laughs, but I don't think it's very funny, not after what I've seen today.

I huff out a breath. "Dante," I start, wanting to ask him about it, wanting to blurt out all my fears.

"Yes, pretty girl?" he murmurs, and I remember the first time he called me that, when he leaned down to check on me after I was almost shot. And each time he calls me that my heart grows larger. Just for him.

I love him. I've loved him since I was seventeen and being around him so much has just made my feelings stronger. Of course I'm going to marry him, because he's the love of my life.

"I love you," I mutter, half asleep, my filters all gone. I know it's soon and he might not be ready, but that's how I feel. Dante goes quiet on the other line.

"I know you do, pretty girl," he murmurs, and that's enough to send me into sleep.

9

DANTE

I listen to Mia breathing on the line before hanging up and heading to bed. I had a long phone conversation with Felicia this morning, since she'd texted me late the night before, asking me to come over.

I'd let her down easy, but Mia has been acting strangely all day. I assume it's wedding jitters, but I toss and turn in bed without Mia there. Have I gotten so used to her presence already?

I should never have opened up to her on the day of my father's funeral, but I'd been emotional and later that night, drunk, and she'd been there to comfort me.

I appreciate that, but at the same time, I don't think it's healthy given that I plan to kill her father and divorce her.

But burning bridges with women like Felicia is the first step to getting Mia (and therefore Luca) to trust me. I need this, and I need to marry Mia, so I need her happy. Not to mention, Felicia is just fun, she we both knew the score from day one.

I finally manage to get a thin few hours of sleep and I

get dressed at home, knowing that Mia will be at the church.

Mia's a strict Catholic (not traditional my ass) and so the wedding will be a long process with a Mass afterward.

Nico serves as both my driver and my best man, and he looks at me curiously as I put on my father's cufflinks.

"Really, *capo*, why are you doing this?" he asks me.

I adjust my tie, looking at myself in the mirror in the small room at the church designated for the groom and groomsmen.

I only have Nico, even though Mia has a maid of honor and three bridesmaids. She's a popular girl, it turns out.

"Because it's what my father wants," I say, and Nico scoffs.

"You've gone against your father many times. Why now do you listen?"

I look over at Nico, needing him to believe me. I could tell Nico the truth, but then he'd try to talk me out of it. He doesn't want me in danger.

"Because he's gone, Nico," I say softly, trying to put all my emotion about my father's passing into it.

Nico slowly nods. "All right, man. I support you. There's gonna be plenty of women crying in the wake of you getting married, though," he chuckles.

I groan. "Don't remind me. I had to talk to Felicia yesterday morning."

"How'd that go?" Nico asks.

"She is having a bit of a hard time letting go, because she doesn't believe I'm really doing this. But she knew it was all just fun and games with us," I say, and Nico looks at me, tilting his head.

"Isn't that always the case with women?" he asks with a laugh, and I shake my head.

"All but Mia," I say, and I can tell Nico isn't convinced, but that's okay. He'll come around.

It's another two hours before Mia's ready, and I'm standing at the altar waiting for her, sighing at her lateness.

The bridesmaids are pretty in pastel-colored dresses, her maid of honor, Marta, dressed in a lavender-colored dress.

When Mia comes down the aisle with Luca, I can't keep my eyes off her. She's wearing a gorgeous, off the shoulder ivory dress with embroidered beads around the sweetheart neckline. The train trails far behind her and she looks up at me, her eyes lined with brown to make the blue irises pop.

My breath catches in my throat. I know that Mia is beautiful, but I didn't expect her to look so...ethereal.

She all but glides down the aisle to my side, and it's all I can do to listen to the priest drone on and on.

Finally, after exchanging our rings, the priest tells us that we're man and wife and I lean down to kiss her, chastely. Mia sticks her tongue into my mouth and I laugh into her mouth as the crowd cheers.

Everyone's handing me envelopes full of cash and gift certificates as we head to the reception area, where Denny is bartending. He's offered an open bar for the wedding, but I'm sure he'll make a lot of that back in tips.

The famiglia is made, by and large, by excellent tippers. And everyone's here, just like they were at Papa's service.

Cousin Leo hugs me hard and congratulates me and Uncle Roberto gives me a check for five grand.

I grin. "It won't bounce, will it?"

He snorts. "Hurry up and cash it before Etta catches on," he whispers, speaking of his shopaholic wife.

I laugh and Mia heads out on the dance floor to dance

with her father. I watch them for a long moment, thinking that they have a very close relationship and feeling guilt hot at the back of my head.

I make my way toward the bar, getting a glass of champagne and gesturing to Mia to come over and help me cut the cake.

As is tradition, she slams it in my face and we both burst out laughing as I do the same to her. It's a lovely wedding, and I'm only half-drunk on champagne by the time we leave for our honeymoon.

We'll be vacationing on the west coast, so Nico takes us to board my private jet.

I have a license to fly it, but I'll be paying someone to do it. It's the night of my wedding, after all, and I hope to join the mile-high club with Mia.

Mia, however, doesn't seem to be in a good mood. Her face is drawn and she looks pale.

"Did you drink too much champagne?" I ask her, wondering if maybe *I* had.

She shakes her head. "No. I just...I need to talk to you about something," she says as we board the jet and sit down.

I call for two more glasses of champagne from the flight attendant I hired, and she brings it right away.

Mia is looking down at her hands, seeming nervous.

"I'm not the type of woman to put up with everything, Dante," she says softly.

I blink at her. "What do you mean?"

"Just, if you're thinking of having mistresses, just know that I won't put up with that," she says, looking up at me. "Divorce is a sin, but I won't live with you as man and wife if you sleep with other women."

I reach over to take her hands in mine. "Mia, I would never be unfaithful to you." Though this is not a love match,

I mean it. "Hasn't your father told you how I've been turning girls down left and right?"

She smiles but only a little. "Yeah, but the fact that girls are throwing themselves at you—"

I scoff. "That's what happens in our line of work, baby. Haven't you seen it happen to your father?"

She bites her lip, nodding slightly. "I guess you're right."

"I am right," I assure her. "And I'm not going to sleep with anyone but you."

She cracks another smile. "You better not," she grumbles, and I kiss her knuckles before leaning forward to kiss her lips.

"Now," I tell her. "Why don't you come and sit on my lap?"

The plane has already taken off, after all, and I have shut the curtains so that the flight attendant can't see inside.

Mia bites her lip again, doing as she's told and sitting in my lap. She's changed into a red sundress and I bunch it up around her hips as she straddles my lap.

"You better not be wearing panties," I murmur.

She grins at me. "Why would I need them? We're on our honeymoon."

"I knew there was a reason I married you," I say before kissing her deeply, putting my hand on the back of her head to pull her closer.

She moans into my mouth and grinds her pelvis against mine. "Have you ever made love on a plane?" she asks.

"I've fucked on a plane before, yes," I admit, making it clear there was no "making love" about it. "But this is the first time I'll be making love on a plane. To my wife."

Mia smiles and shifts to release me from my slacks and I groan as she runs her fingers up and down my length.

"I love you, Dante," she says as she seats herself on my

cock, and I throw my head back, groaning, unable to answer her.

Not that I could answer her honestly, anyway.

I feel an increasingly familiar stab of guilt, but then she starts to roll her hips and I forget everything in my head, just rocking back into her and chasing my own orgasm. It seems like it's been a week rather than just a couple of days that we haven't been sleeping together.

I guess my body's gotten used to having a woman every night, because I feel primal, almost feral, grasping onto her hips tightly as I fuck up into her.

"Dante," she gasps, saying my name over and over, and I start to thrust harder, feeling her tighten around me. When she comes, she's loud, moaning and crying out, and I grin, loving that everyone on board would hear her.

It takes me only a few more thrusts before I come inside her, and she pants against my neck, coming down.

After a few moments, she stands up, wincing a bit, and I frown.

"Are you sore?" I ask.

"No," she says quickly, adjusting her dress. "But I better be before the night is over."

Heat rushes through me.

Mia becomes more and more attractive to me each day. That should probably scare me.

10

MIA

The honeymoon is everything I expected it to be, and our wedding night – well, it's almost perfect.

We end up on the beach after having too many cocktails and I'm giggly and he has his hands all over me. We've found a topless beach and I don't mind doing as the locals do.

The sand gets all over me, but I don't care because Dante's thrusting into me, his breath hot against my neck. He kisses and bites me there, leaving purple blossoms that will sting tomorrow.

I can't stop telling Dante that I love him, and I don't even mind that he doesn't say it back. At least, I don't think I do.

When we're finally showered and sated, lying in bed nude together with no intention of making love again, I turn to him.

"Do you think you'll grow to love me?" I ask him in a small voice, and he looks at me, his eyes glassy from exhaustion and all the alcohol we've ingested that day.

"I think I already am," he murmurs, and he kisses me,

and wonder of wonders, we have enough energy to make love one more time.

I'm on top, this time, with Dante looking up at me and praising me like a goddess. He tells me how beautiful I am, how good I'm doing, and I rock my hips forward faster and faster.

He takes my hips in his hands and bounces me on top of him and that's when I come, hard and fast and sudden. I've lost count of how many orgasms Dante has given me today alone.

When Dante spills inside me again, I don't want him to slide out of me, but it's impossible to sleep that way so I sigh and get off him, putting my head on his shoulder.

When I fall asleep, I don't think life can get any better.

I wake up with sunlight streaming in the window and Dante gone.

Had to make some calls, the note he left on his pillow said. *Work.*

I frown. Is it really work or is he letting some girl down easy? I try to relax my shoulders, thinking that if he's talking to them instead of seeing them, that's a good thing.

I told Dante the truth when I said I wouldn't live with him as man and wife if he cheated. I know that my father has gone astray here and there in his long marriage to my mother, and she's always taught me that when you're married to a goodfella, you have all the power.

I don't know about that, but I do know that I can't put up with it the way that my mother has. I don't have it in me. I'm too jealous, too possessive. I leave marks all over Dante and he does the same, and I love how we belong to each other.

Or at least, I belong to him. One day, I hope the opposite is true.

I sigh, getting into the shower, and I'm sore all over, with bruises on my hips from Dante's fingers, hickeys all over my throat. I smile, looking at them in the mirror after a hot shower that makes my muscles feel less tight.

Dante returns earlier than I thought, bringing room service breakfast – lox and bagels, which I scarf down immediately, starving.

He chuckles at me and eats himself. "What do you want to do today, pretty girl?" he asks.

"Just be with you," I say simply, and he smiles.

"I need to take you on a proper date, so we're going to dinner tonight."

I grin at him. "Funny that you're taking me on a date *after* we got married."

"I guess we're doing things out of order," he teases, patting my head.

I smile and lounge on the bed after eating, groaning. "I'm so tired," I complain.

Dante sits next to me on the bed, looking down at his phone with a frown. "Well, I can always make some more calls, let you get in a nap."

I frown, my eyes popping open.

"Dante?"

He looks over at me with clear hazel eyes. "Hmm?"

"You'd tell me, if there was someone else?"

"There's nothing to tell," he says with a sigh. "I've already told you, any woman I was seeing I've broken it off with. Before we ever got married."

I sigh and nuzzle against his side. "I'm sorry, Dante. I can't help being jealous."

Dante leans down and kisses the crown of my head. "I don't mind you being jealous, but you just have to trust me."

"I trust you," I say, but I'm not all together sure that I do.

Not yet, anyway. I already love Dante, but he doesn't love me back. Dante seems to trust me, but that's what I have issues with. I'll have to learn to trust him.

I let my eyes drift shut, and Dante takes his work calls out on the balcony. He's in and out, but I sleep mostly through it before he wakes me up to get ready for dinner.

"How fancy is the restaurant?" I ask, and he makes a gesture to say so-so with his hand.

I dress in a cocktail dress instead of a gown, a bright yellow one that compliments my olive skin tone and my auburn hair.

Dante whistles as I put on my diamond earrings.

"Look at you, pretty girl," he says under his breath, nuzzling against my neck. He's wearing a black silk shirt and gray slacks that are tailored perfectly.

"Don't do that," I groan. "Or we'll never leave the hotel."

"We can order in," he mumbles, nipping at my earlobe but I laugh and push him away.

"Not tonight," I say firmly. "I want a date."

As much time as we've spent together, I don't feel like Dante and I know each other very well. Other than the night he was upset after his father's service, I don't feel like he's really opened up to me. I hope that I can get something out of him tonight.

Dante takes my hand, and we walk down the beach to a nice seafood restaurant and my mouth is practically watering by the time we're seated.

"This is beautiful, Dante," I say, even though the décor is a little on the kitschy side.

"It's a little cheesy, but it's cute," he says, flipping through the menu. He looks up at me. "You want a drink?"

I blanch. "God, no. I think I drank enough yesterday for the rest of my life."

Dante laughs. "I understand that. Me too."

"At least, let's eat first," I suggest, and he nods, ordering us waters and a shrimp appetizer.

I look at him curiously. "I feel like I don't know that much about you."

Dante spreads his hands. "I'm an open book."

I snort. "I don't know about that."

"Ask me anything," he says, and I tilt my head.

"When did you lose your virginity?"

Dante barks out a laugh. "Fifteen. What about you?"

"Sixteen," I say. "So you see, I'm not a prude like everyone says."

He looks at me. "Does everyone say that?"

I pout. "You haven't heard it around town? All because I like to stay at home mostly, people think I'm stuck up."

"You're not stuck up at all," he says, something glinting in his eyes.

I nod slowly. "I guess maybe I was, for a while," I admit. "After the shootout, I was afraid to leave the house."

Dante gives me a sympathetic look. "I can imagine. You were so young."

I look down at my silverware. "I guess you don't remember me much from that day."

"I didn't for a while," he admits. "For a long time, I didn't think much about it. But when I saw my father's wishes, it all came back to me."

"It did?" I ask, looking up at him.

He shrugs. "You have to understand, Mia, you were just a kid then."

I smile. "I know. I just think...I think that was when I fell in love with you."

Dante's eyes widen. "When you were seventeen?"

I nod slowly. "Is that weird?"

"I think it's very romantic, given I saved your life," he says proudly, and I chuckle.

"You think so?"

"I do," he hums, and reaches across the table to take my hands in his.

The server comes back, smiling. "Newlyweds?" she asks.

"On our honeymoon," I say proudly, and Dante smiles evenly at her, that strange predatory smile I can never quite figure out.

"So, tell me something true," I say suddenly after we put in our orders with the server.

"Something true?" Dante cocks his head.

"Yeah. Something not many other people know."

"My mother was murdered," he says flatly, and I blink.

"Dante, I'm so sorry—"

"And my father was murdered," he continues, popping a shrimp into his mouth like he isn't talking about his parents being violently killed. "And I think it was by the same person."

"Who?" I whisper, leaning forward, but Dante just shakes his head.

"That's business," he says. "And you don't want to be involved in my business, pretty girl."

I sit back in my seat, my head spinning. Does that mean that Dante has some kind of vengeance plot against whoever murdered his parents? That sounds dangerous, and I'm instantly worried.

"You'll take care of yourself, Dante?"

"I'll always protect you," he says, almost robotically.

"That's not what I asked," I say with a huff, and Dante brings one of my hands to his mouth to kiss it.

"I always look out for myself," he says, and it only makes me feel a little better.

The stuffed flounder that I order is wonderful, and Dante gets steak at a seafood restaurant, which makes me laugh.

"You should have gotten lobster with it," I suggest, and Dante makes a face.

"Crab is so much better than lobster," he argues, and I stare at him.

"There's no way you actually think that," I say, in awe.

"I do," he says, smiling so that the little lines around his eyes crinkle. "Is that a dealbreaker?"

"You're entitled to your wrong opinion," I say matter-of-factly, and Dante laughs. It sounds loud and open, from his belly, and I'm not sure I've heard him laugh like that before.

"Dante?" I ask, and he looks over at me. "I know that you've had a hard time since your father died," I start, and Dante's face changes, his brows drawing together.

"Let's not talk about such things at dinner," he says, as if he hadn't brought it up himself earlier.

It's something my father commonly said, and I sigh, thinking about how alike they are sometimes.

"Fine," I mutter, and the rest of dinner goes by easily, with us talking and laughing and Dante eventually coming over to sit next to me, grabbing the underside of my chair and pulling it to him.

It's a move that makes me squeak and makes heat flood my lower stomach.

"I think we should get out of here," I say. "Go back to the hotel."

Dante shakes his head. "No way. I'm taking you dancing."

I raise an eyebrow, grinning.

"You dance?"

He takes my hand, raising it to his lips and kissing my knuckles.

"I'll sweep you off your feet."

I can't help thinking that he already has.

11

DANTE

Mia and I walk the block to the club. It's been years since I've been to the West coast, but I remember a local club called The Peach Pit. It's an upscale place, with a dress code, but Mia is dressed to the nines and I am, too.

There are two bars, one upstairs and one downstairs, and two dance floors, as well. The one upstairs is usually less crowded, so I take Mia upstairs, keeping hold of her hand tightly as we weave through all the people standing around and grinding on each other.

The dance floor remains packed enough that was all the dancing we could do, Mia sliding her ass against my crotch, putting her hands up and into her long hair.

I grit my teeth, taking her hips in my hand and pressing her back against me. We've both had enough to drink at dinner that we don't need more, but after a few songs I'm hot and sweaty and hard beneath my slacks.

"I need a break," I say loudly next to Mia's ear, and she nods, turning to look at me briefly while still shaking her hips. I smile down at her and head toward the bar, ordering us both a couple of waters.

I watch her as I wait for our waters from the busy bartender, sliding her a twenty dollar bill for her trouble. Mia looks gorgeous in that gold colored cocktail dress. It compliments her olive skin and clings to every curve. She's tall in those five inch heels, but I still tower over her. I watch the curve of her waist as she moves, her blue eyes sultry and right on me. I watch as a pair of arms go around her waist, as some guy locks his hands on her belly and Mia's face changes, goes blank.

My smile fades and I abandon the waters, stalking back to the dance floor. My blood boiling.

"You can't cut in," the guy slurs, some idiot with an unkempt beard and a cheap suit.

"You can't touch my wife," I growl, and shove him.

He makes a face and Mia stumbles, but I steady her with a hand on her waist.

She grins up at me as the guy moves away from the dance floor, clearly seeing something on my face that tells him I would win the fight if he started one.

"Were you jealous, baby?" she asks me, wrapping her arms around my neck and swaying slowly against me to the beat of the music.

"Wouldn't call it jealous," I say, speaking loud enough that she could hear me over the boom of the bass. "Just don't like sharing."

She laughs, loud and open, her face lighting up. "I think that's the definition of jealous."

I shrug and smile again, my face still feeling hot with anger. I hate it when guys try to butt in when I am out with a woman, and maybe being married to Mia makes it worse. I take in a deep breath through my nostrils. I can't exactly act the way I do back home, because I don't have the same contacts with the police here. I have a few officers in my pocket back in the city, but here in Los Angeles, I'm likely to get arrested for assault.

Not that it would have stopped me. I have the tendency to snap when I'm really mad, and I was quickly getting to that point seeing someone else's hands on Mia.

Should that worry me?

Mia distracts me by leaning up to kiss me, sticking her tongue through my parted lips and sliding it against mine. I groan into her mouth, putting my hands on her ass and she giggles, moving away.

"Not yet," she taunts. "You're the one who wanted to take me dancing."

She shifts, leaning forward and shaking her ass against my hands, and I can see down her low-cut dress, between her breasts.

"You tease," I murmur, staring at her hotly, and Mia just laughs again, turning around to dance on me for the next song.

I'm going to have blue balls if we stay here any longer and I can't walk out of here with a full erection, so I take her hand and lead her to the hallway of the bathrooms.

"We'll get out of here after I run to the restroom," she says, a shine of sweat across her brow.

I smile at her and watch her go into the bathroom, going in myself to wash my hands and splash water on my face. When I come out of the bathroom, she's nowhere to be found, and I frown.

I walk out back, and she isn't out there, either. She must have gone out the front.

I'm about to go around the corner when I see that asshole who had touched Mia, standing there with another guy who looks just as scuzzy and cheap.

"She had this little yellow dress, her tits spilling out all over the place," he's saying to his friend. "Such a fucking cocktease, you know? Dancing by herself. Then her asshole of a boyfriend walks up and gives me attitude, so I pushed him off me."

"So, where's the girl?" the other man asks.

I freeze in place, rage rushing over me. I don't know what it is that pisses me off so much, something about the nonchalant way he called her names, talked about her tits. He has no right to talk about her that way. Mia is my *wife*, even if it's in name only. There's no fucking way I'm letting him get away with that, especially after he had the gall to touch her.

I walk over to him and as he turns to me, I grin at him and punch him directly in the face.

His friend yelps and backs away, clearly not one to break up a fight.

The scuzzy guy falls to the ground, holding his cheek.

"What the hell? Who the fuck are you?"

I don't answer, hitting him again and again until my knuckles split. I've broken his nose and busted his lip before Mia puts her hands on my shoulders, pulling me away.

I'm breathing hard, sweating, and I have blood on my knuckles, part mine and part his.

"Dante, stop!" Mia yells. "Someone's going to call the cops."

"Let them," I snarl, pulling away from her and spitting in the guy's face. He whimpers. "No one talks about my wife's tits like that. No one calls her a fucking tease."

He whines out an apology, begging me not to hit him anymore and it just disgusts me. He hadn't even fought back. I kick him in the ribs once, twice, before Mia tugs me toward the car she'd called for us desperately.

I finally turn toward her, panting.

"Dante," she whispers as we hurry to the car. Her face looks blank and worried, and I figure she's going to be mad.

The driver opens the back door quickly, his face pale as he looks toward the guy in the parking lot.

I give him a hard look and he swallows visibly as we get in and he closes the door, hurrying to the driver's side.

"Fuck, Dante," Mia murmurs, and when I turn to her to apologize, she climbs into my lap, kissing me hard and hungry.

I kiss her back just as hard, putting my hands on her hips, thrusting up beneath her. I'm already half-hard in my slacks. She pulls away to take a breath and I latch on to the base of her throat, making a mark there.

She moans, rocking her hips toward me, her dress riding up to bunch around her hips. Her thighs clench around me and I surge up beneath her again.

"You're mine," I mumble against her skin. "No one touches you but me."

"Yes," she breathes. "All yours."

I keep marking her throat, leaving a row of red marks, and Mia gasps, her body trembling as I work her over.

I pull away to rip down the top of her dress, tearing it in the middle so that her breasts bounce free. I put my mouth on one nipple, sucking and nipping, and then the other, and Mia moans so loud that I'm sure the driver is blushing.

I'm grateful that the limo has plenty of room, because I need her *now* and we're both wearing too many clothes. I shift her so that she's lying on her back and tug up her skirt, noting that she's not wearing any panties and groaning low in my throat.

I slide my fingers through her slick heat, pressing two up inside her and she arches her back, whispering my name over and over. I love the way it sounds like a prayer.

"Look at me," I demand, and Mia's blue eyes pop open. "Want you to know who's making you feel this good."

"You, Dante. Always you," she moans.

Heat floods through my body and my balls tighten up, aching because I need to be inside her right now.

I fumble with the buckle of my slacks, the alcohol fuzzing my brain, and finally free myself, guiding myself into Mia with one hand.

She rocks her hips forward and I don't fuck her slow and steady like I usually would. There's something primal in me, something that needs to make her mine, and I thrust into her hard and fast, quick strokes just chasing my orgasm.

Mia doesn't seem to mind, she's making all manner of incoherent noises as the driver pulls onto the freeway. I rock into her faster, harder, watching where we're joined together, loving the lewd sounds it makes when I pump in and out of her.

I look down at her face, her blue eyes wide and glassy, full mouth parted, and my hips stutter as she cries out.

"I'm coming, Dante!"

I can feel it, feel the way her walls clench around my dick, and it feels like heaven and I'm only a stroke behind her, shuddering as I fill her up with my seed.

Mia lets out a long breath like she's been holding it when I pull out of her. She sits up shakily and rubs along her neck where I've left a necklace of hickeys.

"I'm going to have to wear a turtleneck in summer," she teases, and I make a displeased noise in the back of my throat.

"Absolutely not. I want everyone to know you're taken. I want them to know you belong to me and only me," I growl, and Mia gives me a hot look.

"You could have gotten thrown in jail back there," she

says, but there's no edge to her voice. She almost sounds excited.

I shrug. "I would have gotten my lawyer to get me out of it. No one talks about my wife that way."

Mia grins. "Your wife," she says, as if in awe. "I'm really your wife."

A pang of guilt shoots through me. She's clearly more and more attached to me, and I can't let myself get close to her for real. For one thing, I don't do that. I don't get close to women. They're useful for certain things, but at the end of the day I've got responsibilities, ones that I can't push to the side. And they are a liability I don't need. A weapon against me.

I just nod, plastering on a smile, and the driver stops us in front of our hotel room.

I hate playing with Mia's emotions, but I have to remember that this is what I need to do. Mia is right, I really could have gotten arrested, and it would have been a couple of days before I could get out. I've lost track of what really matters, just burying myself in Mia's body, and I can't give up on my goal.

I need to avenge my father, and Mia is just a way to do that. Nothing more.

12

MIA

Today we return home, and I can't stop thinking about last night in the limo. It was so *hot,* the way that Dante had stood up for me, the way he'd attacked that guy because he touched me. I know that Dante is a dangerous man, and that could have gone a lot worse than it did, but something about it excites me.

It means that he cares about me. It means that he wants me to be his, and that makes me so happy. I'm excited to take the trip home, thinking that Dante and I may make love on the jet again, and in preparation, I wear a sundress without any underwear.

Dante wakes up and immediately starts to pack, though, keeps checking his phone and texting someone. I frown. I know that he has work to do and that he might have some things to take care of, but I feel rejected after our intimate night.

"Work?" I ask him as we get onto the jet.

"Hmm?" He looks at me blankly, distracted.

"Is it work?" I ask again, irritated.

"Oh. Yeah," he says simply, looking back to his phone and sending another message.

I huff out a breath as I sit down. I know I'm being a bit of a brat and that he's a busy man, but I guess I thought I'd get more than just a few days of the honeymoon period, even if we're going home.

He's on his phone the entire four-hour trip and I end up just reading and entertaining myself. I keep reminding myself that I know who I married and that he's the Caputo, of course he's busy. I should be grateful that he took time off for the honeymoon.

But when he gets up to go to the bathroom, I can't help glancing over at his phone. I pick it up slowly, looking down at it. I don't care what he does for work. I'm just worried that he's talking to a woman. I see a notification from him that says, "It's over," and it's a number, not a contact name. I frown.

I glance toward the bathroom and he's still in there, so I take my phone and quickly call the number.

"Hello?" a female voice answers, and my throat tightens.

"Sorry, wrong number," I mutter and hang up, tears burning at the backs of my eyes.

It's not common for members of the famiglia to work with women, so I know that it's probably that same girl I heard him talking to back at the house. My heart drops. At least it says it's over and he doesn't have her contact name saved. Maybe that means that he's done with her?

But why is he still texting her on our honeymoon?

I hate feeling like this, hate feeling jealous and insecure. But Dante only married me because it was his father's dying wish. It isn't because he's in love with me. And he hasn't said I love you back, even though I've said it multiple times.

I can't help feeling like a fool.

Dante returns and immediately looks at his phone again. He finally sits it down, looking over at me with a smile.

"Do you want something to eat when we get home?" he asks. "We could go by and have dinner before going home."

I shake my head. "I don't have much of an appetite."

Dante frowns. "Are you feeling all right?"

"Too much booze on the honeymoon," I say, cracking a smile, and Dante laughs.

"Poor baby," he croons. "Come sit on my lap and I'll make you feel better."

I force myself to smile. "Not this time. I'm feeling really tired," I lie.

Dante takes it in stride, and I close my eyes against the tears. I don't know how to deal with this, how to talk to him about it.

It's not my business who he was with before me, but it's certainly my business who he's with now. It should be only me. But he's told me that's the case, and I have no real reason not to believe him.

"I've got work to do all evening," Dante says.

Of course he does. That doesn't surprise me, but there's a big part of me that worries it's not work at all – that it's that *woman*.

When we arrive at home, Dante goes to shower and invites me, but I decline, feigning being tired and hungover.

I am tired and hungover, but that's not the reason I don't go into the shower with him. I'm just feeling rejected and stressed, and I need some kind of outlet.

When Dante comes out of the shower wearing just a towel, I bite my lip, regretting my decision for a moment.

"How long will you be gone?" I ask.

Dante shrugs. "A few hours."

"I'm thinking about going to see Marta."

He frowns. "Nico's driving me, and I don't want a new driver driving you around. Can't she come here?"

I think about it for a moment. Marta hasn't seen the mansion yet, at least not since I moved in.

"All right," I say with a smile.

Dante puts a stack of cash on the nightstand. "Order in whatever you want."

"We might raid your liquor cabinet," I tease.

He smiles and suddenly I feel slightly better about everything. His smile really lights up the room, dimples popping out of his cheeks.

"What's mine is yours, pretty girl."

Dante walks toward me and kisses me softly before leaving the house, and I feel stupid for ever doubting him. Just because he let some girl down easy doesn't mean that he's still seeing her, right?

Maybe I'm being paranoid.

"You're absolutely not being paranoid," Marta says, sipping her martini. "Dante has a hell of a reputation. I'd be worried, too."

I stare at her. "Why would you say that to me? Now I'm stressed out!"

Marta laughs. "You were already stressed out."

We are both a little tipsy since I grabbed a bottle of top shelf vodka from Dante's liquor cabinet and we've been drinking vodka martinis.

"Do you know who he was seeing before me?" I ask, even though I don't really want to know.

"There was this bottle blonde named Felicia," she says. "They were pretty hot and heavy for a while."

I swallow hard. *Felicia.* I've seen her around. She's kind of a wiseguy groupie and I know a lot of them. They are always around the famiglia in the area. But Felicia is a blonde bombshell. She has a perfect hourglass figure and she's around Dante's age.

"Not Felicia," I groan. "She's so pretty."

"She's a nobody," Marta says disdainfully. "She's not even full Italian."

I sigh. Marta can be a bit snobby about her full Sicilian heritage. "Neither am I," I mutter.

Marta's eyes widen. "Sorry, Mia, I didn't mean it like that," she backtracks. "I just mean she doesn't have connections, not like we do."

Our fathers are both Caputos, and now I'm married to one, so I understand what she means. But it doesn't make me feel any better about Felicia and Dante.

"Make me another drink," I demand, and Marta does so.

"Do you think he's sleeping with her still?" I ask after another drink, my words slightly slurred.

Marta shrugs. "I dunno. You know how wiseguys are. They have a wife and a mistress and two on the side."

"Like my father," I whine.

I know that he's cheated on my mother, that he's had relationships on the side and full-time mistresses. He loves my mother, but that's just the lifestyle. I don't want that with Dante. I want to be the only one. I'm not the type of woman who can deal with my husband cheating on me.

"Mine too," Marta points out. "I just think that's what we have to expect, right?"

I wrinkle my nose. "That's not what I want to expect. I want him to love me and only me."

She gestures to the hickeys all over my neck. "I think he does definitely love you," she laughs.

"That has nothing to do with love," I argue. "It's just because some guy touched me at a bar."

Her eyes widen. "Shit. What did Dante do?"

"He beat the hell out of him," I admit. "It was almost scary."

Marta raises an eyebrow. "But also kind of hot, right?"

"So hot," I agree, giggling. The alcohol has gone to my head.

She sighs. "I wish I had what you had. All I have in Vincenzo Gallo sniffing around."

I grimace. "Not him."

Vincenzo Gallo is next in line as Caputo of the Gallo family, and he's disgusting. He started sniffing around me when I was only sixteen, and I've always found him awful and creepy. He's not nearly as handsome as Dante, and not half as respectful.

"Right? He went from you to me like I'm supposed to think he's in love with me, or something," Marta complains.

"You don't have to date him," I point out.

She sighs. "My father is urging me to. He says it'll help us gain territory. But I'm tired of being a tool to be used, by everyone."

I understand exactly how Marta feels. Even with Dante, it seems like my father married me off in order to gain power. He never asked me how I felt about the situation. It turns out that I've always had a thing for Dante, and I think he's an honorable man, but my father hadn't cared about that.

I suppose he would never marry me off to someone like Vincenzo, because he's disrespectful, but I still feel like Marta does sometimes: a tool to be used.

"What about Rocco?" I ask, and Marta sighs heavily.

"You know I'm madly in love with him, but he's not in line to be Caputo, so my father won't even entertain it. I just sneak around and see him that way."

"You live a fascinating life, Marta," I say, and she snorts.

"I don't know about that."

I get up unsteadily and make us another drink and we chat about men and our family lives and what we've recently purchased. I give Marta a little tour around the house.

"We should go skinny dipping," she suggests, and I grin at her.

"You're reading my mind," I tell her, and we jump into the pool nude, laughing and splashing each other.

I have a great time with Marta, and I certainly drink too much. She passes out in the guestroom after a while and I'm not tired, so I sit down on the couch, watching television.

It hasn't occurred to me what time it is, but it's pretty late, and Dante still isn't home. I can't be angry with him about it – I know that Dante has a lot of late nights.

But I can't help but wonder – what if he's with Felicia? What if he's kissing her right now? Lying her down on her bed?

The thought of it makes my stomach feel sick, and I lie down on the couch. I think that I'll probably never get to sleep, at least until Dante gets home, but between the alcohol and the travel fatigue, I drift off quickly.

I dream about Dante lying next to a buxom blonde, holding her in his arms.

13

DANTE

I make it home before midnight and I'm hoping that Mia is awake and tipsy because I know she'll be frisky. I've been thinking about her all night, about that row of marks I left on her neck, how I want her to show them off.

I know that I was cold to her this morning, but all day I've been talking to Felicia. She's been taking the news that I'm breaking it off hard, and drinking too much. It can't be helped, but she's a friend and I want her to be okay.

Finally, I just deleted her number and told her it was over, and she hasn't contacted me again. Maybe she got it through her head.

I tried my best to let her down easy, after all.

When I pull into the garage, I see Marta's car already in there, and assume they're having a sleepover.

I walk into the house and Mia is sleeping on the couch, her hair damp. She's wearing a pair of yoga shorts and one of my T-shirts and she smells like vodka.

I smile, crouching near her and brushing her auburn hair from her face. "Mia," I say softly, and she groans and rolls over.

I pick up her arm and let it fall back down. She's out, so all my plans to make love to her tonight are out the window.

I chuckle and scoop her up into my arms. She has the presence of mind to wrap her arms around my neck and bury her face into my chest. It makes my heart feel warm, and then an immediate feeling of guilt washes through me.

She isn't her father. I hate that I'm playing with her feelings like this, but it can't be helped.

Can it?

I walk upstairs and put her in the master bedroom, covering her up. I plan to crawl in next to her right after I undress, but as soon as I start to unbutton my shirt, my phone rings.

"Hello?"

"It's Vincenzo," the voice on the other end of the line says.

"Gallo? What's up?"

I don't talk to Vincenzo Gallo much, but his father was an ally to my father. The Gallos and the Riccis have been on good terms for decades, and so I trust him.

"I heard gunshots out by one of your businesses. The dry-cleaning place?"

I curse under my breath. "When?"

"Just about fifteen minutes ago. I wanted to give you a heads up."

"I'll be there in a few minutes."

I sigh, looking down at Mia for a long moment, longing to get into bed with her and sleep. I'm tired from the trip and from working all day, but I guess it isn't meant to be.

I call Nico and he picks up right away, always ready.

"*Capo?*"

"There's something going down at our dry-cleaning business," I say quickly. "I need you there. I'll meet you."

"Be there with bells on," Nico answers.

I'm grateful for Nico, he's more like a brother to me than just an employee, and I feel a bit better that I'll have backup as I head downtown.

I park illegally and jump out, cursing when I see that all the glass has been shattered.

Nico's already there with his gun out, checking the perimeter.

"They've cleaned out," he says after a few moments.

"Fuck," I curse again, and then I walk inside, stepping over broken glass and turning off the blaring alarm. "Call Richie," I tell Nico, speaking of the cop that has helped me and my father for the past decade.

Everyone's got a few cops in their pocket. Richie's been a friend to the Riccis for years. His mother and my father had a thing back in high school, and Richie and his family have been loyal to us.

Nico does as I say as I survey the damage.

On the back wall, there's an upturned hourglass spray-painted on the sheet rock.

Great.

The upturned hourglass is the symbol of the Lorenzo famiglia, and I'm not surprised that Luca tried to destroy my business. He wants to take over my territory, and I'm not going to let that happen.

I seethe, wanting to call Luca right away and ask him what the hell he's doing. We're supposed to be on good terms after I married his daughter, but I guess we're not.

"Gallo's here," Nico warns me, and I turn around and Vincenzo is stepping through the glass at the front of the store.

"Fucking Lorenzo," Vincenzo says.

I've never quite liked Vincenzo. He's kind of a creep

with women and once he came on to Felicia while we were together and it pissed me off, but overall, he's been helpful.

He's a little guy, standing about five-foot-seven, and although he's only a couple of years older than me, his hairline is receding.

I look down at him. "Why would he do this? I just married his daughter, for God's sake."

It doesn't really make sense.

Vincenzo shrugs. "Maybe his guys didn't get the memo."

I hum. That could be it, but I don't think so.

I already have plenty of reason to hate Luca Lorenzo, but now I'm even more irritated. This isn't on the same par as killing my father, but it's a pain in my ass.

"Maybe you should call him," Nico suggests.

"Call him for me tomorrow," I command. "Set up a meeting."

It's time for us to have a talk anyway.

Nico helps me start to clean up while Vincenzo stands there like a log until I throw a broom at him.

Richie the cop shows up and he whistles at all the damage.

"What the hell happened here?"

"Luca Lorenzo," Vincenzo pipes in, and I give him a hard look. He shrugs and goes back to sweeping up glass in a half-assed way.

Vincenzo seems to love sticking his nose in my business, but I guess since he alerted me to the situation, I can't be an asshole to him like I want to be.

I want to be an asshole to nearly everyone right now. I had plans to go home and make love to Mia and instead I'm here cleaning up like a goddamn janitor.

I throw the broom down, thinking I have men who will do this for me.

"Call in a few guys," I tell Nico. "I'm not doing all this work."

"Anything you say, *capo,*" he says, walking back out into the street.

Richie takes a few notes. "I'll keep some guys patrolling around, but there's no real evidence."

I pointed at the upturned hourglass. "Isn't that evidence?"

Richie shakes his head. "Everyone in the city knows that's Lorenzo's mark. Anyone could have done it."

Richie has a good point. It could be anyone that wants me to think that it's Lorenzo, but why? I don't have beef with any other of the famiglias in this area.

Unless they have beef with me and I just don't know it.

I run a hand through my hair, frustrated.

"I saw Ricardo's Mercedes," Vincenzo pops up. Ricardo Rossi is Luca's right-hand man.

Richie nods and takes down a note. He's mostly useless unless one of the famiglia gets arrested, but for show I have to have a report put down.

And for the insurance.

"You should just torch the place," Vincenzo says, throwing down his broom.

"Keep your opinions to yourself," I snap, and Vincenzo holds up his hands.

"Just a thought, *capo,*" he says, but I don't like the way he says it. It sounds almost condescending.

"Why are you so interested in my property, anyway, Vince?" I ask, taking a few menacing steps toward him.

Vincenzo backs up, keeping his hands up. "I don't!" he insists, his voice going high-pitched and frightened.

I scoff. Vincenzo is a coward, always getting his men to do the dirty work. I keep trying to like him because he's helped me now and again, but it's hard to change my opinion.

"I'll get out of your hair," he says, and exits the building.

Nico comes back around, making a wide berth around Vincenzo. He has the same opinion of him as I do.

"This feels off, boss," Nico says, and I nod.

"It's fucking weird, that's for sure," I say. "Right after my honeymoon? Which Luca paid for? It doesn't make sense."

"Vincenzo ringing the bell makes me suspicious. I'm going to get a couple guys to follow him," Nico says, and I nod, relieved.

Nico knows when something smells fishy, and this smells like high tide.

14

MIA

I wake up at daylight and something feels off. The house feels strangely empty, and I peer out the window and see that Dante's daily driver isn't in the garage.

I get up and go downstairs to see if Marta is up yet. When I don't see her, or anyone else for that matter. I sit down on the couch and put my head in my hands. After that dream (nightmare) I had, I don't know what to think about Dante being out all night.

I know he probably has work backed up, but all night long?

As I sit there, thinking I should make myself a glass of water for my hangover, Dante comes stumbling in the door.

I look up at him, glaring at him.

"It's fucking seven in the morning, Dante. Where have you been?"

"Working," he mumbles, throwing his keys on the counter.

"Don't you think you could have called?"

"You were passed out drunk. Didn't think you'd care,"

he snapped. "Don't bite my head off just because you're hungover, princess."

I seethe. I hate being called princess because it suggests that I'm spoiled. Maybe I am, but Dante doesn't have to say it. Besides, I've been worried all night.

"Were you with someone else?" I ask softly, and Dante scoffs.

"I'm getting real tired of this argument, Mia," he says roughly, heading up the stairs without even looking at me. "I had a long night."

"I bet you did," I mutter, following him up the stairs, but instead of arguing with me, he just shuts the bedroom door in my face.

I want to scream. I stalk back downstairs to see if Nico has returned and he hasn't. That's it. I'm taking my car and getting the hell out of here.

I text Marta to let her know to meet me at the local coffee shop. It's only a few blocks down the road, one of those upscale ones with coffee milkshakes.

Once I'm behind the wheel of my car, I realize that I shouldn't be driving. I still feel dizzy and nauseous and I'm probably still under the influence. I groan and get out, deciding to walk. I put on my running shoes and take off, walking fast because I'm angry.

I know that the nightmare I had is probably affecting me and that's why I'd been so worried about Dante being with someone else. I just can't stand the idea of it, and it's driving me crazy.

As I'm walking, a sportscar pulls up next to me and a man hangs his head out the window.

"Hey, sexy," he calls, and I roll my eyes, walking faster.

I hate being catcalled, but it's something I've dealt with

several times while walking alone. I ignore the car completely.

"Don't ignore me, gorgeous," the guy drawls, moving the car closer to me and I step further off the sidewalk.

"Leave me alone," I mutter, taking my purse and holding it. There's mace in there, and I'll use it if I have to.

I've used it before, and I can take care of myself. My father always told me to be prepared, and I am.

I pull out my phone and call Marta. She doesn't answer.

"Pick up, pick up," I whisper, and finally she does.

"Hello?" her voice sounds cracked and hoarse.

"Marta," I say quickly and loudly, so that the guy knows someone is on the other line. I keep looking to the cars driving by him but no one seems to care.

"Why are you calling me from the next room? Are you that hungover?"

"I wanted you to meet me at the coffee shop," I say calmly, and then I pause. "Some asshole is following me."

"Shit," she curses. "Stay on the phone with me, I'll be right there."

I take in a deep breath. It'll be okay. Marta is close enough that she'll be there soon.

"Just stay on the line," I tell her.

"Of course. Fucking men," she curses.

The guy veers over closer and tries to grab me, and I spray the mace right in his face, fumbling to get it out of my purse and dropping the whole bag, including the phone in my left hand.

"Mia?" she calls, and I can't answer.

I curse and try to pick it up while the guy yells and stops the car.

Another man gets out of the back and grabs me around the waist. I scream and kick and bite down on his arm. He curses but then the driver, who I didn't get with the mace as much as I meant to, puts a burlap sack over my head.

Then someone punches me in the face and everything goes black.

When I come to, someone's tying me to a column and all I can see is the inside of the burlap sack. I start to hyperventilate, thinking that I'm about to be killed.

"Calm down. Boss wants you alive and kicking," someone says near my ear, and I shudder, pulling away.

I wish the sack was off my head so I could spit in his face.

I feel myself panicking but I keep reminding myself that Marta knows where I was when I got taken. She knows that I'm in trouble, and she'll tell Dante and my father.

"You're going to die," I tell the guy.

"Not before boss has his fun," he says, as if he's not concerned about death at all.

Jesus. What does that mean? I'm terrified as to what might happen to me, but Dante or my father (or both) are coming.

I take deep breaths in through my mouth since the burlap is over my nose.

"Can I have some water?" I ask meekly, not wanting to make the kidnappers mad. I don't recognize any of the voices, but I can tell two distinct voices at least.

"Fuck off," the man who tied me up says.

"The boss wants her feisty," the other voice says. "You better give her some."

I listen closely so that I can hear the guy get closer and wait, and then I kick out my foot, connecting with something.

"Ow, fuck!" the man who tied me up says.

I feel a small moment of victory before pain explodes in my face and my head goes fuzzy as the man hits me again.

"You're going to bruise her up!" the other man exclaims, ripping off the burlap sack.

"Now she can see us, you idiot!" the man who tied me up says. He's tall and lanky while the other guy is short and stocky. I try to memorize their faces.

"You're both going to die," I say calmly, and the guy snarls at me, reaching out to hit me again. I flinch but the other guy pulls him away, crouching down to look at my face.

He stays far enough away so that I can't kick him.

"She's going to have a black eye. *Capo* is going to beat your ass for that," he says.

"They're coming for me," I say again, but my voice comes out shaky.

"Yeah, yeah," the mean one says, pulling the sack back over my head.

I hadn't had time to memorize my surroundings, but I appear to be in a warehouse of some kind. The bright lights overhead are visible even through the sack on my head.

They've brought me here to kill me, I think, and my breath starts to come short all over again.

All I can do is hope that Marta comes through.

"Vincenzo won't like this," the nicer guy says, and my breath catches in my throat.

Vincenzo is a creep and I know what he's going to want to do to me.

"Dante's going to kill him," the nicer guy mutters, and I hear the other guy scoff.

"He'll take care of Dante just like he took care of his parents."

My eyes pop open inside the burlap sack. That means

that Vincenzo had Dante's parents killed. I would have never expected the Gallos, a low-level famiglia, to make that kind of move. They must want the Ricci territory, that's the only explanation.

It seems like I've been here for days, although I know it's probably only been a few hours. I'm thirsty and I wiggle around, calling out to the men.

"I need water!"

"You don't need *shit*, princess," the mean one says. "The boss will be here to pick you up any minute."

Panic tightens my throat again. I know that Vincenzo is going to hurt me, and hurt me badly.

Please, Marta, I think.

I have no way of telling time but in a bit, my mouth is so dry I can barely make saliva. I wiggle and try to get loose from the ties, but it's not enough. They're too tight.

I'm starting to lose hope.

A door bangs against a wall. Fuck, is that Vincenzo coming for me?

I start panicking and then start the gunshots.

I scream and duck my head, thinking of the first time I was involved in a shootout. Dante had come to save me then, and I hope against hope that it's him, now. Please, please, please be Dante.

I can't wait to see him.

That is, if I survive the shootout.

15

DANTE

I'm sleeping peacefully when the phone buzzing on the bedside table wakes me up. I groan and start to throw it across the room, but given what happened last night, I need to be on guard.

I pick it up instead of destroying it like I want to.

"What?" I bark.

"Dante, it's Marta," Mia's friend says, speaking too quickly. "I think someone's taken her."

I bolt upright in bed. "What? Where? She's here," I say, getting up and walking downstairs to find her. She's not on the couch, and her purse is gone. Fuck.

"She told me she was walking to the coffee shop and some guy was sniffing around her."

"What guy?" I demand, my heart leaping into my throat.

"I don't know," she says, her voice shaky. "But I came to get her and all I found was her purse and her phone. It's broken. She's gone, Dante."

I curse and want to slam my phone down on the table.

Why had she left the house? On foot, no less? What the hell was she thinking?

Instead, I take a deep breath. "Call Luca, tell him what you know. I'll find her," I say, and hang up the phone.

I immediately call Nico, who has spent the day watching the store. "Nico. Come back to the house."

"I've been watching the store—"

"I know. Come back to the house *now*." I command.

While I wait for Nico, I pace around the house. Marta would call Luca and I'll have more backup. I hate that I have to work with the old man, but Mia is missing.

My heart is pounding too fast. Who the fuck would have taken my wife?

I should be concerned that I keep thinking of Mia as my wife, but I can't worry about that right now. All I can do now is get to her.

Nico finally arrives and I walk out with him. We drive out toward the coffee shop and I yell for Nico to stop as I see something glinting.

When I get out of the car, my heart drops when I see it's Mia's broken phone and her designer purse. The mace is lying outside of it. Marta must have left it there for us to find, in case there were any clues.

"Shit," Nico curses.

"Who the fuck would do this?" I growl.

Nico raises an eyebrow. "I didn't want to say this before, Dante, but I've heard that Vincenzo has a thing for Mia. Or at least, he did, back when she was a teenager."

I whirl around and glare at him. "Why wouldn't you tell me that?"

"I didn't want you to kill him," Nico says simply.

"Fuck!" In a fit of rage, I kick Mia's purse further into

the ditch. I'll buy her a new one. I'll buy her anything, as long as I can find her. My heart feels like it's in a vice.

"I'll call around, find out where they do business," Nico says quietly, watching me heave in breaths and almost break down.

I brought Mia into my life, and it's my fault that she's been taken. If I had been home. If I had taken the time to talk to her this morning...

I get back into Nico's car as he makes some calls, rubbing my hands over my face.

I don't know what to do. I hate feeling helpless. I keep getting flashbacks of not being able to reach my dad and then finding out that he was murdered.

"There's a couple of warehouses downtown. They can't be far," he says, and gets into the car.

"Drive like you stole it," I tell him, and Nico nods curtly, listening and hauling ass to the first warehouse.

He creeps around the perimeter with his gun and I take mine out of the back of my pants, heading straight for the front door.

"No one's here," he says, but I kick in the door anyway, looking around the warehouse.

Nothing. Fuck.

Nico puts a hand on my shoulder.

"It'll be okay," he says. "Listen, Marta called right after it happened. It has to be around here somewhere."

We hit jackpot on the second warehouse, a crumbling, abandoned one. It's huge and it's taking Nico too long to go around the perimeter so I sneak to the side, peeking in one of the broken windows.

Two men are speaking in hushed tones, and when I look past them, I see a woman tied to a post with a bag over her head.

Mia.

I growl in the back of my throat and meet Nico at the back.

"She's in there," I say. "Cover me."

"Wait—" Nico starts, but it's too late, I'm already breaking into the back door.

The second I get in, Nico starts shooting, and I duck, firing my gun at the first guy once, and then twice. The first bullet hits him in the chest and the next in his throat, and he goes down, covering the gushing wound with one hand.

The other guy sprints toward me as if he's going to tackle me, but Nico shoots him in the leg as I get him point blank in the face and he falls to the ground, dead.

I don't realize there's a bullet in my shoulder until I lift up my arm to take the bag off of Mia's head and pain rockets through me.

"Who did this?" I ask, cradling her face with one hand, looking at her bruised cheekbone.

"I...I don't know," she says, looking away from me. There are tears streaming down her face, and I swear to God, I'll kill Vincenzo the second I see him.

She stares at me blankly. She looks traumatized and all I want is to take her into my arms but my shoulder feels numb, my whole arm aching.

"Pretty girl," I croon as Nico unties her. I'm planning to scoop her up into my arms but I can't, Nico puts a hand on my good shoulder.

"You're hit, *capo*," he says. "We need to call the doctor."

"Get her home first," I say, and I'm starting to fade in and out. I look down and blood is soaking my white shirt.

"Dante," Mia whispers.

I black out for a moment, but when Nico helps me up, pain shoots through my shoulder and I cry out. He all but carries me to the car, leaving Mia to trail behind us. I don't like it. I want her home. I don't want her to see any of this.

"You have to put pressure on the wound," Nico orders. His voice seems to be coming from very far away.

Mia presses a handkerchief against my wound and I grit my teeth not to scream. Nico's looking at the back of my shoulder.

"It's a through and through, thank God," he mutters, before getting me into the car. Mia gets in with me, in my lap and pressing the cloth against the still-bleeding wound.

Mia's pale face and blue eyes are the last thing I see before I black out.

16

MIA

Dante keeps passing out and I've never been so scared in my whole life. There's no way I can tell him about what I heard about Vincenzo and his parents. If he got hurt trying to save me, he might get killed trying to get rid of Vincenzo.

The only way to keep pressure on the wound is to sit in his lap and face him and I see his eyes roll back into his head over and over as he struggles to maintain consciousness.

My face aches all over but I can't even think about it right now. All I can think about is Dante.

When we arrive at the house, Nico carries Dante in over his shoulder and I jog next to them.

"He needs whiskey or something, we're going to have to stitch it up if the doctor doesn't show," Nico says, and I felt myself go even paler.

"In the liquor cabinet," I point toward it and Nico runs over, grabbing a bottle and handing it to Dante, who was semi-conscious.

Dante takes a big swig, and then another, chugging almost a fourth of it.

"Fuck, it hurts," he groans as I press the handkerchief

harder on the wound. He's covered in blood and now my hand and arm are covered, too. How much blood can a man lose?

"Oh, God, it's still bleeding so bad, Nico," I whimper.

"I know," he says softly. "The doc is on his way. Just stay with him, I'm going to try and find some gauze."

"In the upstairs bathroom," Dante croaks.

Nico runs to get it, quickly, and returns with the bandages. "Can't find rubbing alcohol. We'll have to use the whiskey."

I look over at him, panicked. "Can't we just wait for the doctor?"

Nico shakes his head. "We don't have time. He's losing too much blood."

"I'll be fine," Dante says, but his words are slurred and I don't like that. The whiskey hasn't even had time to hit his system, so it's from the blood loss.

I've seen him injured before, but not like this. Never like this. I've never seen anyone this injured before, and there's something tight in my chest.

What if Dante doesn't make it? What if the doctor doesn't get here in time.

"Fuck, I need a needle and thread," Nico says, not thinking clearly.

"I've got one upstairs," I manage. "On the table, there's a bag with my sewing supplies."

What kind of thread and needle did you use for skin, anyway? Did the color matter? I'm thinking nonsense, but I can't help it.

"Dante," I say, slapping his cheeks lightly. "Stay awake for me, baby."

His eyes roll forward again, his hazel eyes glassy.

"I'm up," he mumbles, shifting in his seat and then

crying out at the pain in his shoulder. I'm in his lap, still pressing against the wound and when he moves, I lose my grip.

Fresh blood spills down his shirt through the bullet-sized wound. "Where the fuck is the doctor?" I yell, and Nico runs down the stairs.

The doorbell rings and I'm so grateful that I could have passed out. I'm glad I don't, though because I have a job to do. I have to keep pressure on this wound and I have to keep Dante awake.

I slap him again, harder, when his eyes roll back in his head.

"Ouch," he complains, but his eyes look a little clearer and I take a breath that I'd been holding.

"Just look at me," I tell him. "Just keep looking at me."

"I'm looking," he slurs, focusing on my eyes.

The doctor comes in. I know him. He's the same doctor that my father uses. His name is Jimmy Sawbones, or at least that's what everyone calls him.

He rushes to Dante's side, crouching down next to him.

Jimmy takes my arm. "You've got to let go so I can look at it."

I shake my head frantically. "No, no, it's too much blood," I mumble, but he is stronger than me and gently but forcefully removes my hand.

He rips off Dante's shirt, pulling it off of him as Dante grits his teeth, almost yelling.

"No bullet," Jimmy murmurs, looking at the wound with a discerning eye. "But too much blood. Nicked an artery." He looks over at Nico. "Hand me my bag," he says, nodding toward where he'd dropped it on the floor.

Nico opens it and brings it to him and Jimmy keeps one hand on the wound while he rummages around in the bag.

He's got a needle and thread, probably better than what I had in my little sewing kit.

He looks at me.

I remember suddenly the last time I'd seen him. My father had been stabbed between the ribs and he'd stopped breathing as we waited, my mother sobbing at his side.

Jimmy Sawbones had stuck a needle into his lung and reinflated it, saved his life.

He's a good doctor, I tell myself. *He'll save Dante.*

"I need you to hold pressure while I thread the needle," he says, and then looks up at Nico, all business. "And for God's sake, man, put on your flashlight so that I can see what the hell is going on."

Nico fumbles with his phone but gets the flashlight on and I put pressure on the wound again as Dante mumbles out curses.

"What's he had?" he asks Nico.

"Whiskey," Nico answers.

"That's not going to be enough." He tosses Nico a bottle of pills. "Two of these now, one every six hours after."

Nico nods and shakes out two pills, shoving them in Dante's mouth and offering him the whiskey bottle again. Dante drinks deeply from it and swallows.

Jimmy takes the needle in hand and threads it, first try, tying it off with his teeth. Then he moves my hand out of the way and digs into the wound. I wince but I can't look away, it's like watching a train wreck.

He digs around in the wound and Dante howls, his hands clawing onto the chair arms for support. "Fuck, that *hurts!*"

"Good, I'd be worried if it'd gone numb," Jimmy replies easily, cracking a smile.

I blink at him. Is that a joke?

After what seems like thirty minutes of Dante writhing on the chair while Jimmy gets hold of the artery, he says, "Got it," calmly and puts the needle inside the wound. I can't see anything but blood and tissue. I have no idea how he found the artery.

Nico takes off his belt and gives it to Dante, who puts it between his teeth. He's sweating and I dab his forehead with the bloody handkerchief, having nothing else and not wanting to leave him.

Dante passes out when Jimmy gets the stitch in, and the belt drops to the floor.

"Dante?" I call, my voice high-pitched with panic.

"It's for the best," Jimmy says softly. "This next part isn't pleasant."

He starts to stitch the wound but what I don't realize until he gets Nico to help him sit Dante up is that there are *two* wounds, one where the bullet went in and the exit wound.

He stitches the back one in record time because Dante is coming to.

"The pills will make him loopy," Jimmy tells me. "Keep an eye on him. It's going to take a couple of weeks to heal, but he won't be up and around tonight."

He starts to wind gauze around Dante's shoulder. Dante's still out of it, his eyes rolled back, eyes slightly open.

"He-He's going to be okay?" I stutter, and Jimmy smiles softly.

"He'll be fine, kid," he says, patting my shoulder. "And you did good. You're a good wife, Mia."

I nod slowly, feeling like I'm somehow floating outside of my body. I feel out of it just as much as Dante, I guess from the stress.

Jimmy looks at me intently, at the bruises on my face.

"I need to check you out, too. Nico, get out of here, I need to lift her shirt."

Nico blushes slightly and leaves the room.

Jimmy lifts up my shirt and I wince. I look down and there's a purplish bruise all the way across my abdomen, from the bottom of my ribs to my navel.

The doctor palpates there and I cry out.

"You've got a busted rib. Not broken all the way through, just cracked," he says, and takes a bandage out of his bag. He starts to wrap my abdomen, right below my breasts and down to my waist. It hurts at first but when he's done, I feel like I can breathe again.

"That's so much better," I marvel, and Jimmy nods.

"Keep that bandage on unless you're in the shower. No lifting, for at least a week," he warns. "I'll come back and check on you in a few days."

"Jimmy," I say, tears suddenly springing to my eyes. "I don't know how to thank you—"

"Your husband will thank me with money," he says gruffly, and picks up his bag, walking toward Nico.

Nico comes back into the living room.

"What can I do to help?" he asks, and I'm so grateful to him if I wasn't married I would have kissed him.

"Help me get him upstairs," I say. "We both need a bath."

Nico nods. I pat Dante's face softly, and then a bit harder.

He finally rouses, looking at me. "What happened?" he asks, his voice slurred and hoarse.

"You got stitched up. You did good, baby," I say, my voice choked with tears.

Nico tugs him up by his good arm and puts himself under his good shoulder, walking him up the stairs. Dante cries out a couple of times when he has to brace himself on the banister, but we very slowly make it to the bedroom.

"I need to rest here," Dante says. "Fuck the bath."

I giggle almost hysterically at his words and sit down hard next to him on the bed.

Nico exits the room quietly, as if he were never there at all.

Dante looks at me, his eyes glassy still from the booze and the medication, not to mention the shock.

"Are you okay, pretty girl?"

The way he's asking about me when he's the one who's hurt warms my heart. "I'm fine, Dante," I assure him.

"Your face," he says, cupping it with his right hand, his good hand. "They hit you."

His voice sounds mournful instead of angry.

"Yeah, a couple of times. I kicked one of them in the nuts," I say, smiling a little.

"Atta girl," he says with a weak smile. "I feel like shit," he admits.

"You lost a lot of blood."

Dante looks down at himself as if for the first time. His bare chest is stained with blood and it's pooled in his belly-button, drying there. "Shit. I guess I did."

I smile a little at that.

"Let me help you get cleaned up," I say, and he doesn't complain as I undress him, starting with his boots and slacks and then tugging down his boxer briefs.

I need a shower, too, but I'll handle that after Dante is all cleaned up. I hate having the stink of the Gallos' warehouse on me, the way that man had hit me. I keep reminding myself that he's dead, shot in the throat. I'd seen him as I walked out, him and the nicer guy, too.

"Gallo did this," Dante says suddenly, and my eyes dart to his.

"We don't know that," I say slowly.

Dante stares at me intensely. "Tell me what you do know, Mia."

I swallow. I don't want him to go off half-cocked, going after Vincenzo. If he goes after him injured, then Vincenzo will have the upper hand.

"I don't know. They were just talking about their boss. I didn't get a name," I lie. "I was so scared..."

I trail off, a sob catching in my throat.

Dante puts his good arm around me, pulling me close and putting his forehead against mine.

"I'm going to get whoever did this to you, Mia. I swear to you."

"That doesn't matter right now," I say. "All that matters is getting you better."

I slowly disentangle myself from him and walk to the bathroom, wetting a washcloth and putting a little soap on it. I keep the water cool, but not freezing.

When I place the cloth on his skin, he winces as I get closer to the wound, but I just wash around it in a wide berth, telling myself he can clean himself in the shower when he's better. If I hurt him, I'd never forgive myself.

It takes three rags and several trips to the bathroom, but I get him mostly clean. The blood has traveled down to his waist on both sides.

Dante sways on the bed slightly and I frown at him.

"You should lie down. Get some rest," I tell him.

"Don't want to," he slurs. "Want to see you."

I smile, my heart clenching in my chest. He's so sweet when he's drugged and shot. I push at his good shoulder lightly and he falls back onto the bed. Then I take his legs and swing them over the bed and he wiggles under the covers.

"Come to bed with me," he says, and I gingerly climb into bed. He watches me. "You're hurt somewhere else. Where?"

He tugs at my shirt and I show him the bandages on my ribs.

"I'll be okay in a few days," I promise.

"I'm going to torture Vincenzo for days before I kill him," Dante seethes.

"I told you, don't worry about that. Not right now. Like I said, I don't know who it was."

"It seems awfully fucking convenient that Vincenzo kept me out all night by telling me about the storefront shooting, and then you get kidnapped the next day."

"It was all my fault," I mumble, looking down, tears welling in my eyes. "I shouldn't have left the mansion alone."

"You shouldn't have," Dante agrees, but then he frowns at my tearful expression. "But it's not your fault. Nothing that happened was your fault."

He pauses, looking intently at me.

"What?" I ask.

"Did he—" he hesitates, gulps loudly, and I shake my head vigorously.

"They kept saying the boss was coming but you and Nico showed up before he did," I explain.

"Thank God," Dante breathes.

I can see from his face that he's not going to let this go, that I have to tell him about Vincenzo, but I'm leaving the part out about his parents. He may listen to me when I ask him not to go after Vincenzo over me, but the death of his parents? That's a different story.

"I think it was Vincenzo," I admit. "I heard one of them say his name, but I can't be sure."

"Nico said he used to have a thing for you. Why didn't you tell me that?" His voice doesn't sound demanding, just curious.

I shrug. "I don't know. I don't like to think about it. I was just a kid, like sixteen, and he asked my father if he could take me out. Papa beat him nearly to death, but he never stopped sniffing around and asking about me."

"Fucking creep," Dante curses, and I nod.

"I can't be sure it's him, but he's certainly always been after me," I tell him.

Dante nods. "Thank you for telling me, pretty girl."

His voice sounds exhausted. I know that he must be tired. I'm lying on his good side so I snuggle up next to him and he puts an arm around me.

"Get some rest," I tell him, but he's already softly snoring.

Now it's me that's awake, alone with my thoughts.

It takes me a long time to fall asleep.

17

DANTE

I wake up feeling groggy as all hell with Mia cuddled up next to me, sleeping fitfully. My arm has fallen asleep around her and I wince as she flops around.

"Mia," I call softly. "Wake up, pretty girl."

She stirs and opens her blue eyes. They look bloodshot. I grit my teeth, thinking of all the ways I'm going to destroy Vincenzo Gallo.

It'll start a turf war, because we've always been on good terms, but I couldn't care less. Coward bastard, not even showing up to take Mia himself.

I guess I'm grateful. If he'd been there, I'd have killed him on the spot.

This way, I get to have a little fun.

"I'm awake," she mumbles, sitting up and rubbing her eyes. "What time is it?"

"I don't know. I can't really move," I say, chuckling, and Mia's eyes widen.

She scrambles off the bed. "I'm sorry, did I hurt you?"

I shake my head. "No, no. Everything's fine. How are your ribs?"

She's holding her side, so I know they hurt.

"They're okay," she lies.

I frown. "I'll call Nico. He has those pills Jimmy gave him."

"I don't need any pills," she argues.

"Just one," I tell her. "So that you can get some rest. I know you didn't sleep well last night. You were tossing and turning."

She winces. "I just kept having these dreams..."

"I know, baby," I say softly, and reach for my phone on the nightstand with a grimace.

Mia grabs it up and hands it to me.

"Don't stretch, you'll pop a stitch," she scolds.

I smile and take it from her. "Thank you, Nurse Mia," I tease.

"Damn right," she says with a pout, and I wish she was closer so I could kiss her.

I call Nico and he picks up right away.

"Boss?"

"Where are you?" I ask.

"Downstairs. I crashed on the couch in case something happened in the night."

"Good man," I hum. "Do me a favor and bring those pills Sawbones gave me."

Nico hangs up the phone and his footsteps sound as he comes up the stairs.

I have to make a note to raise his pay. He saved my life with that cover fire and getting me back to the house. I never would have made it alone.

Nico tosses the pills onto the bed and I fumble with them to get one out for Mia, handing it to her.

She takes it dry and then goes into the bathroom, shutting the door.

I look over at Nico and he looks back at me. I know that he knows what I'm thinking. I know he knows that I want to get Vincenzo *yesterday*.

"Not today, *capo*," he says quietly. "You need to stay with her."

I nod. "I know. I'll wait a few days. Keep an ear out, will you? I don't want him skipping town."

Nico nods and quietly leaves the room. I struggle to sit up, my shoulder on fire. I dry swallow just one of the pills myself, wishing I had asked Nico for a glass of water.

Mia, bless her, brings one from the bathroom and I gulp it down hungrily. She doesn't even blink, going to refill the glass. I drink half of that, too. Blood loss sure takes a lot out of a man.

Mia had done so wonderfully last night. She hadn't panicked when I'd been shot, just did what she needed to do.

"Thank you," I tell her, and Mia tilts her head, frowning.

"For what?"

"For taking care of me last night."

She scoffs. "Of course. You'd do the same for me."

It turns out that I would. When I'd heard that she'd been taken, my heart had leapt into my throat and stayed there until I saw her face again, bruised though it might be. I know that should worry me, but I'm still floating on whiskey and painkillers and adrenaline.

I'll think about all those difficult things later, after I've taken care of that yellow-bellied fuck Vincenzo.

Going after a young girl, not even eighteen. It's a wonder that Luca didn't kill him back then. I've already decided to call Luca, tell him what I know. I hate to work together with the old man, but at the same time, I need to find who did this to Mia and I need to get rid of him so that nothing like this ever happens again.

"I need to call my father," Mia says, as if reading my mind. "I'm going out onto the balcony. Call if you need me."

I nod, but I don't plan on calling her unless I absolutely have to. She's already seen me at my worst, seen me weak and nearly sobbing in pain.

I don't want anyone to see me like that, especially not the woman I married, even if it is just a marriage of convenience. Wiseguys are strong, especially made men, Caputos, and I had to take that on after my father died, whether I was ready or not.

I suppose now I've been tested.

I still want Luca Lorenzo dead for what he did to my father, but if I can use his influence to get Vincenzo Gallo and wrap my hands around his neck, I'll suck it up and do it.

I struggle to my feet and make my way to the bathroom, looking at myself in the mirror. I look much paler than my usual olive tone and blood's blossoming on the front of the bandage. I turn around to look at the back, but there's no blood there. That's a good sign.

I know Jimmy will be by today or tomorrow to check up on me, and it doesn't seem like I've popped a stitch, so I turn on the shower and get in, making sure to keep the stream away from the wound. The bandage will get wet, but Mia can help me put another one on.

I sigh as the hot water hits my skin. It feels amazing because I'm sore all over from my muscles tensing with the pain of last night's ordeal.

The shower is quick because I can't stand for too long without swaying – those pills that Jimmy gave me sure pack a punch – and I crawl back into bed after drying off, not bothering to get dressed.

Mia's outside on the phone with her father for a while longer, and my eyes are drifting shut when she comes in.

"You leave me any hot water?" she jokes, and I nod, smiling.

"Should have waited for you," I comment.

"I don't think you're in any shape for shower sex," she teases.

I bark out a laugh. "Maybe not."

She slowly unwinds the beige bandage that Jimmy must have put on her, and the bruises all over her torso are in full view.

I curse. "Who did that to you?"

"One of the guys grabbed me around the waist to put me in the car and I fought him. Probably broke my own damn ribs," she mutters.

"Good girl," I praise. "I hope you kicked him in the nuts."

She laughs and it sounds slightly out of control. Mia's not okay and I can tell just by looking at her.

"That shootout, the one when you were a kid," I start, and Mia looks at me blankly. "Was that the only time you've been in danger?"

"Yeah, I think so," Mia says softly. "My dad always protected me from the worst of it. I've seen him get hurt, but that was the only time I was in the middle of it."

"So, this morning was hard for you," I say simply, not asking, just stating a fact.

Mia smiles weakly. "Not as hard as it was for you."

I scoff. "That's bullshit. I got hit by a stray bullet. You were taken and didn't know what was happening or how you were going to get hurt. I'm so sorry that I was a dick when I got home."

She looks away. "Where were you all night, anyway?"

"Vincenzo called me, told me that someone shot up my dry-cleaning business," I tell her. "When I got there, he pulled up right away. I should have known he was up to something."

Mia's eyes widen. "Do you think he did it?"

I nod. "To get me out of the house. They just got lucky that you happened to be walking to the coffee shop." I give her a hard look. "No more of that, okay? Never leave the house without me or one of my men. Preferably Nico."

Mia bites her lip. "I'm sorry, Dante. Marta was asleep and I just wanted to get out of the house. I was feeling overwhelmed and as if I couldn't breathe. I needed air and a change of scenery, since I was mad, but I'd been drinking...it was stupid."

"It wasn't stupid. You have every right to walk wherever you want, baby, but when you're you and you're married to someone like me..."

"I have to be careful," she finishes quietly.

I sigh. "I'm not scolding you. I was just terrified when you went missing."

She looks back up at me with bright blue eyes. "You were?"

"Of course I was," I say softly, keeping her gaze. Maybe it's the drugs or the adrenaline, but I find myself wanting to open up to her, wanting to tell her...

Tell her *what?*

There's nothing to tell. She's just a girl, and we've been spending a lot of time together. Sure, it's flattering that she loves me so much, but I'm on a mission to kill her father. This isn't going to last.

I lick my lips, my mouth dry again, and take the water glass and drain it.

Mia goes into the shower but it's a quick one and when she gets back out, she looks pale. I'd been dozing off so I sit up, frowning and grimacing at the pain in my shoulder.

"Hurts?" I ask her. "You should wrap it back up."

She nods slowly and takes the bandage, wrapping her ribs up fairly tight. I can tell that she's holding her breath, but she lets it out slowly when she's done wrapping them.

"Better now," she says with a slight slur. Mia's eyes are going glassy, so I reach out and take her wrist.

"Come back to bed, pretty girl," I croon to her, and she crawls back against my good side. This time I turn to face her instead of putting my arm around her.

She puts a hand on my face, looking into my eyes. "You're really okay?" she asks hoarsely.

"I'm really okay," I promise. "I'm just sore and tired."

"Me too," she agrees, sniffling. "I was just so scared that you would die, Dante. There was so much blood..."

I brush my nose against hers before kissing her softly. "But I'm okay now."

She cracks a smile, still sniffling. "You owe Jimmy Sawbones a debt."

"More than one," I drawl.

"Is he the one that stitched you up when you saved me the first time?" she asks.

I nod. "Along with a few other times."

Mia reaches around to my back, to the knife scar just below my ribs.

"Who did this to you?" she asks. "The knife scar."

"I don't know," I say honestly. "I got jumped outside of a bar. Could have just been a mugger or something, I guess, but they didn't take anything."

"My father has the same wound," she says thoughtfully. I blink. "What?"

"My father. He has the same scar. Someone knifed him between the ribs, just about an inch higher than yours. Punctured his lung."

"Jesus," I mutter.

That doesn't sound right. Maybe I was wrong all along about getting mugged. If there's one Caputo with a knife scar, that's one thing. If there's two…

It's a pattern.

I tell myself that I'll speak to Nico about it when Mia and I get some more rest.

Her eyes are drifting closed and I can't help myself from kissing her closed eyelids. She smiles and then starts to breathe heavily and evenly, going back to sleep.

There's something wrong with my heart. Maybe it's from losing all the blood, but it's beating too fast as I look down at Mia. She still has the marks I'd left on her throat on our honeymoon.

It feels like she's holding my beating heart in her hands, and I don't know what the hell to do about it.

18

MIA

Dante doesn't mention Vincenzo for a full week. Jimmy Sawbones comes back to check on us the next day. I don't take another pill after that first day. It made me sleep a whole twelve hours, and I don't want to be dead to the world if Dante needs me.

Jimmy says that Dante's stitches are healing well but warns him not to pop them, and that my ribs should be healed in a couple of weeks. He's not even sure they're broken, just bruised. They still hurt like hell.

Nico's at the mansion almost all the time, rattling around downstairs while Dante and I stay upstairs and order in food. Marisa, the housekeeper who lives downstairs, brings us up some homemade Italian lasagna the second day, and Dante eats so much I think he's going to be sick.

Looking back later, that week is almost like a second honeymoon. Dante's doting and sweet, cuddling me in bed when I'm sore, and even though he can't move around much without pain, he orders me anything I want.

It's nice.

Dante's been getting up the past couple of days and heading downstairs, trying to get his strength back. He's been doing well, and I'm happy for him, but at the same time I'm terrified that he's about to go after Vincenzo and get hurt again.

But I know this bubble in time when it's just us is going to come to an end. I'm nervous all the time, and I'm still having nightmares. And now my stomach is rioting.

I brush my teeth in the hall bathroom so that Dante won't notice. I don't need him worried about me. I know it's just the stress and the trauma from the kidnapping.

"I'm going out today," he says, and my chest tightens.

"Why?" I ask, and it comes out sounding whiny and petulant.

Dante chuckles. "I have to leave the house sometime, pretty girl."

"You're hurt," I argue. "And so am I."

"We're on the mend. And I'm not leaving you alone. Nico will be here."

That does make me feel a bit better, because I know that Nico is his right-hand man. Dante doesn't make big moves without Nico, and so maybe he's just doing some other, less dangerous work.

I'm about to ask where he's going and what time he'll be home when Nico knocks on the open door, shielding his eyes just in case we aren't decent.

"Hi, Nico," I say, and Nico drops his hand, smiling at me.

"Hi, Mia," he says.

Nico's a sweet guy. He's been known as a bit of a womanizer, but what wiseguy hasn't? Nico isn't even a made man, just half Sicilian, and he's handsome.

"I'm going to go out for a meeting," Dante says, and a

look passes between them that I don't like.

It's just like with my father and his right-hand, Ricardo. They seem to have a telepathic connection sometimes, after working together for so many years.

I don't like that I can't read what Nico and Dante are saying.

"I'll stay here with the missus," Nico says. "We'll order some pizza from Fatty's."

My stomach rumbles. On top of being nauseous, I seem to be starving.

Dante laughs. "Seems like she'd like that."

"Dante," I start, going to ask him more questions, but then Nico clears his throat.

"Before you go, *capo*, you have a visitor."

Dante raises an eyebrow. "A visitor?"

Nico nods, his face blank.

I stare at him. "Who is it?"

"Felicia Nunez," Nico says, and my heart drops to the floor.

"What the hell is she doing here?" Dante mumbles, and pushes past Nico to go down the stairs.

Nico follows him and I follow them both, struggling to keep up because of my ribs aching. I want to see this, Felicia Nunez coming in *my* house to see *my* husband.

Dante pauses at the bottom of the stairs.

Felicia is standing there, dressed casually in a pair of cut-offs and a tank top low enough that I can almost see her nipples. I grit my teeth.

"Dante," she breathes. "I just had to see with my own eyes that you were okay," she explains, taking a couple of steps forward.

"I'm fine," Dante barks, looking into her face. "You need to leave."

Felicia pouts. "But I just got here."

"And now you're just leaving," Dante says, taking her arm roughly and pushing her out the door.

"You're really okay, Dante?" she asks before he closes the door and he sighs.

"I'm really okay," he says in a kinder voice, and then shuts the door in her face.

I glare at him. "Why is Felicia Nunez visiting you?"

"Mia, don't start—" he begins, but I'm seething.

"Women can't just come into *our* house like that," I snap.

"I didn't let her in, Nico did!" Dante argues, trying to make light of the situation but I'm not having it.

"Dante, who is she to you?" I demand to know.

"She's... a friend," he hedges.

"What kind of friend? A friend with benefits?" I say wryly.

"Not anymore," he says, taking a few steps toward me and putting his hands on my shoulders. "There's only you, pretty girl."

I soften at the look in his hazel eyes, but I still don't like it. I'm fuming at her wearing that skimpy shirt, too. Who dresses like that to go visit someone ailing?

"I've got to go," he says gently, and kisses my forehead. "Please stay with Nico. Promise me."

"I promise," I say, and I'm telling the truth. After what happened, I don't even want to go anywhere by myself.

Dante presses a wad of cash into Nico's hand. "For whatever she needs."

Nico nods and then Dante walks out the door.

I look at Nico. "You wanna play cards?" I crack, and Nico laughs. He looks much younger when he laughs.

An hour later, he's creaming me at gin rummy and I

throw down my cards.

"Remind me never to play cards with a criminal," I joke, and Nico chuckles.

"I'm better at stud poker," he says.

I raise an eyebrow. "How much better? I've got a pretty good poker face."

"Let's play."

"Quarters," I suggest, and Nico reaches into his pocket and pulls out a handful of various coins.

"How about nickels?"

I laugh and nod and we start an ante.

I win all his coins in under an hour and Nico throws down his hand in disgust.

"Remind me never to play poker with a mafia princess," he jokes.

I smile at him. "How long have you known Dante?" I ask.

"Shit, since we were kids. His father was like a father to me too," he tells me.

I cock my head, interested. "And you started working for him..." I trail off, hoping he'll continue.

"As soon as I became his best friend, and I became aware of the family business, I always protected him," he says flatly.

"Where was your father?" I ask.

"Died when I was twelve," he answers.

"Jesus, I'm sorry," I tell him softly and Nico shrugs.

"Nothing to be sorry for. That's life, right?"

I frown, thinking that in their line of work, Nico and Dante are risking their lives every day.

"What's the deal with Felicia?" I ask suddenly, since Nico is being open with me.

Nico looks away from me. "Felicia who?"

I scoff. "The bimbo that just came in here fawning over my husband. Tell me, Nico. Were they together?"

Nico groans. "You're lucky I don't like to lie to pretty women."

I smile tightly, showing my teeth. I've picked it up from Dante.

"They had...a thing."

"What do you mean, a thing?"

Nico shrugs. "A thing. Off and on, nothing serious."

"She seems serious about it," I mutter.

"She was a lot more serious than the boss, that's for sure," Nico admits.

"And now?"

Nico gives me an even look. "Now, there's no thing. The boss is married to you. End of story."

I can tell that he's not going to say anything further, and so I push back from the table and deal us another hand.

I start feeling worse and worse as we play and eat pizza, and eventually I excuse myself to go to lie down.

Nico props himself up on the couch downstairs.

I lie face down on the bed but the momentum of bouncing makes me dizzy and I get up and lurch to the bathroom, throwing up in the sink.

"Ugh," I mutter, washing it down with water from the faucet.

I need a friend, so I call Marta.

"Mia," she answers. "How are you, girl?"

"Like a bus ran over me," I admit.

"Why?" she asks. "Are you worse from your rib pain? Maybe you should ask for an x-ray."

"It's not my ribs. I think it's something I ate. Or maybe from just the stress of everything that happened," I explain. "I've been sick twice already today..."

Marta pauses so long I think she might have hung up on me.

"Marta?"

"Mia, are you sure that's all it is? When's the last time you had your period?"

I blink, thinking back. "I don't know. Who keeps up with that sort of thing?"

"People who don't want to get pregnant," she says wryly.

I blanch. "I'm not pregnant. I can't be. Dante and I have only been married..."

We've been married a month, but we first had sex two weeks before that. And thinking back, I don't think I've started my period since I've been with Dante.

"Shit," I curse.

"You need to get a test," Marta says firmly.

"Come bring me one," I plead.

"No way, sister," she says quickly. "Papa has me sheltering in place after what happened to you."

"Then how am I supposed to get a test?" I hiss.

"I don't know! Be creative. And call me back."

I look on Postmates and sure enough, there's no pregnancy tests available at the local Walgreens.

I sigh and walk downstairs.

"Nico, I need you to take me to the store."

"Boss doesn't want you leaving the house if we can help it, " he says firmly. "I'll get you what you need and have Alberto keep an eye on the house."

Alberto is one of Dante's drivers.

I swallow hard. "But, Nico, it's lady's stuff," I argue.

Nico's ears go red. "I don't mind," he mutters.

Damnit.

"Fine," I mumble. "I need you to get me a Gatorade and a pregnancy test."

Nico blinks once, twice, then he just looks at me.

"What kind of Gatorade and what brand of test?"

I groan. "Lemon lime and I don't know, the most expensive one." I pause. "And don't go reporting back to Dante. This might be just me stressing out over nothing."

I'm not pregnant, I keep telling myself. *It's just stress. Marta's just making me paranoid.*

"Got it," he says, and pulls out his phone, presumably to text Alberto.

Alberto arrives in just fifteen minutes and I'm downstairs staring into space when Nico calls that he's leaving.

"Thank you," I say blankly and Nico gives me a little salute.

Alberto doesn't talk much on account of someone ripped out his tongue (a story I heard from my father years ago), and so we sit there in silence before Nico returns.

I snatch the bag from him the second he walks in the door. "Don't you say a word," I warn, and Nico puts a finger to his lips, smiling.

I head upstairs to the master bathroom, taking the test while my head is still spinning. Does Dante even want kids? We haven't talked about it.

We haven't talked about much of anything, now that I think about it. We're too busy being unable to keep our hands off each other.

I stare at the test for a full minute before stalking back into the bedroom, pacing around until the five minutes are up. The timer goes off on my phone and this strange feeling of dread and excitement washes over me.

Positive.

I start to hyperventilate.

19

DANTE

I can't believe what I'm about to do. I can't believe I'm about to partner up with the man who killed my father, but we have a common goal: protecting Mia. I didn't tell Mia where I was going because I knew she'd be upset. She's been so worried about me since we've both been recovering, and I'll admit, the stitches in my shoulder still pull like hell. I'm hoping that I won't pop them today, but I can't make any guarantees.

I sigh when I arrive at Luca's, running a hand through my hair. By now, I'm supposed to be coming here to kill him, not to have a friendly meeting where we discuss teaming up to kill Vincenzo Gallo. I haven't let go of my end goal. Quite the contrary. I've just been forced to play a longer game that I thought I would have to.

Usually, one of Luca's men's at the door, but today, Luca himself opens it, smiling at me, his suit jacket off and his sleeves rolled up. There's blood, looking almost like lipstick stains, on his collar.

"You started without me," I drawl, and Luca throws back his head and laughs.

"Couldn't help myself," he admits, leading me to the back of the house. There's a steel door, one that I've never noticed before. Of course, I haven't taken a real tour of the house or anything, but it seems pretty secluded, in a small room meant for something like laundry in the back of the house. Luca may have had it built specifically for this, for all I know.

"You already picked him up?" I ask, slightly disappointed. I'd wanted to see Vincenzo's face when I showed up.

Luca shrugs. "Thought I'd save you the time."

He starts to put in the key code outside the door and I put a hand on his shoulder.

"Wait just a second," I say. "I want to ask you something."

"What's that, son?"

I plaster on a fake smile, hating the way he calls me that now. "One of my businesses was shot up, vandalized. Vincenzo called me about it, told me he heard the gunshots, and saw Ricardo's car fleeing the scene. When I got there, your insignia was spray-painted on the wall. The hourglass."

Luca scoffs. "Dante, you know Vincenzo is a liar. He probably did that to keep you out of the house while he went after Mia."

I nod. "I figured as much, but I had to ask."

"That sonofabitch," Luca mutters. "Trying to put a wedge between me and my son-in-law."

No, I think. *You did that yourself when you put a bullet in the backs of my parents heads.*

But I keep on that fake, plastered smile. "All right," I say. "Let's do this."

Luca puts in the key code and the door slides open to

the right, and a muffled scream comes through the doorway. I peer inside and Vincenzo is tied to a chair, rocking back and forth but making no progress. The chair is nailed to the ground. There's a drain, curiously, close to the back of the tiny room, just barely big enough to contain a grown man.

"It's my panic room," Luca says with a smile. "You like it?"

Panic room isn't quite the right word. I would call it a torture room, but I grin at him. "I do," I confess. I especially like the drain in the floor to help with the cleanup, after.

I may have to consider getting one for my place, but I think Mia might protest.

Vincenzo's got crusted blood around his nose and mouth, and he's gagged.

"I only hit him a couple of times," Luca says almost sheepishly, and we both walk into the room together. I have to duck slightly to get through the doorway, but it's surprisingly roomy enough to fit us both in height, anyway. We're standing shoulder to shoulder, looking down at the panicked Vincenzo.

Luca rips off the duct tape, and Vincenzo yelps as it tears skin off his lips. Then he removes the rag from Vincenzo's mouth.

"Listen, Luca, if you're pissed about the dry-cleaning joint—" Vincenzo starts and Luca slaps him across the face, open handed.

Vincenzo grunts but doesn't scream, gritting his teeth, blood crusted around his mouth and nose, his lips red and chapped.

"I don't give a fuck about the dry-cleaning joint. You took my *daughter*," Luca growls, looking down at Vincenzo disdainfully.

"I don't know what you're talking about," Vincenzo

says, and just looking at his lying, ugly face makes my blood boil.

I punch him in the nose and hear the crack as his nose breaks. My shoulder screams with pain but I don't care. Vincenzo makes a sound like a wounded animal, snuffling and whimpering.

"I want to do the honors," I say, and Luca shrugs as if he doesn't care one way or the other.

"All right," Luca says. "But don't make it easy. I want to watch."

Vincenzo trembles. "I haven't had anything to do with Mia since Lorenzo hurt me last time I tried to date her," he said, his voice nasal and choked.

"Do you think it'll do any good? Lying to me?" I say, and to save my shoulder, I lean back to kick him in the chest. All the breath comes out of him in a rush and blood sprays on my shirt. I look down, disgusted, lowering my boot back down to the floor as Vincenzo gasps.

I look around the panic room and there's a little medical table full of instruments. Some of them look very interesting. I pick up a pair of pliers, and Vincenzo yells something incoherent, barely able to breathe.

I change my mind, and Vincenzo relaxes. Then I pick up a small scalpel and lean down, holding it to his right cheekbone.

"What are you doing?" he whispers, his voice liquid.

"I think I might have to cut off this ugly, lying face of yours," I comment idly, and Vincenzo bucks in the chair. It rocks and clangs, but Vincenzo isn't going anywhere.

I slice into his skin, just slightly, and watch the blood trickle down his face. Vincenzo starts to scream.

I look back at Luca and he's got his arms folded across his chest, watching with a slight smile on his face. It's a little scary, truth be told. It won't be easy to kill Luca Lorenzo, but I've never imagined that it would be.

I slice down to his chin and stop, admiring my handiwork.

"It's not my fault," Vincenzo spits out, glaring up at me with his beady eyes. "She was just walking down the street in a pair of shorts, her ass hanging out. Not my fault you married a whore."

Rage boils through me and I go after him with the scalpel, but Luca pulls me back, putting a hand on my shoulder. I barely note the movement when he raises his gun, cocks it, and shoots Vincenzo point blank in the face. I blink, looking down at the tiny hole in his forehead.

"No one calls my baby girl a whore," Luca snarls,

I watch as a drop of the blood drops down onto the floor, swirling slowly down the drain.

"Now," Luca says, clapping his hands together. "Would you like some tea?"

I smile weakly and Luca shuts the door of the panic room. I assume he has a cleaner, just like I do, and he'll call him up after tea.

Luca leaves me alone in the living room while he makes the tea. When he returns, he has a crisp white button-up shirt folded in one hand and a tray with a teapot and tea cups in the other.

"Thank you," I murmur. Luca hasn't changed, still covered in blood.

"I figure you don't want the missus to know what we've been up to," Luca says with a chuckle.

I shake my head. "She's been worried about me."

Luca nods. "My missus worries about me, too. That's why I send her away to her sister's when I have business. I send all of the staff with her, tell her I need her well taken care of. I don't want any one flapping their jaws about what I do in my own home."

I nod slowly, sitting down for tea.

We chat idly for a few moments, Luca just sitting there, covered in blood, and I change my shirt before I leave. I keep my shirt crumpled in my hand but Luca stands up and takes it from me.

"I'll have it dry-cleaned," he says with a grin.

I realize, belatedly, that he's making a joke about my dry-cleaning business being destroyed, and I bark out a surprised laugh.

If Luca Lorenzo hadn't killed my father, I may have liked him.

20

MIA

I look at my phone for about the twentieth time since Dante has been gone, my heart pounding in my chest. Has he gone after Vincenzo anyway? After telling me that he wouldn't? I can't be sure.

Nico's still here, so I don't worry quite as much as I would if he wasn't. Dante doesn't do much business without Nico, they're partners as much as they are friends. But I suppose he could have taken Alberto instead...

I've been upstairs, looking around the rooms up there to see which one would be the best nursery, but I decide to go downstairs. Nico is in the kitchen, drinking a beer.

"Nico, I want you to level with me," I say, trying to keep my tone light.

Nico looks at me, his gaze suspicious. "About what?"

"Is Dante going after Vincenzo Gallo?" I ask, looking him right in the eye.

Nico has absolutely no change in expression. "Not that I know of," he says easily.

I narrow my eyes. I can't tell if he's lying, and I have a

lifetime of experience with shut-down wiseguys. Nico must be a hard shell to crack.

"So, why isn't he home yet?"

Nico shrugs. "Our line of work, sometimes stuff takes a while."

I open my mouth to argue but then I hear Dante's key in the front door and I rush into the foyer, looking him over.

He doesn't appear to be injured, but he looks tired and he has an envelope in his hand.

I soften, realizing that Dante really did just have other business. I almost feel bad for not trusting him. "You look like you had a long day, baby," I croon, kissing his cheek.

Dante nods, wincing as he puts the envelope in his pocket and takes his suit jacket off. There's no blood blooming through his shirt, though, so I suppose everything's okay.

Nico leaves quietly like he does every night when Dante goes home. I'm sure he's annoyed he gets stuck babysitting me every day, but he has a room here for a reason, and Dante always says he doesn't mind.

"Let's go get you a bath," I suggest, and Dante smiles at me weakly.

I head up the stairs and he follows me more slowly, clearly favoring his injured shoulder. I run the bath and he walks in behind me when it's half full, undressing and lowering himself into it with a grunt.

I look at the wound on his shoulder and there is some blood soaking through the bandage, but it's not too bad. At least he hasn't popped a stitch.

When I remove the bandage, though, it's red and irritated-looking. I make a displeased sound in the back of my throat.

"Baby," I say softly, not quite scolding but almost, and Dante smiles sheepishly.

"I still have to go to work," he explains.

"I know," I say quickly. "I just wish you could have taken more time off to heal."

I have thought about how to tell Dante about the baby all day, but right now, Dante needs comfort. He's had a long day and he's still injured, and I want to be here for him before stressing him out with my sudden pregnancy.

I take a washcloth and wet it, putting some soap on it before rubbing it across his back.

Dante groans low in his throat, and even though it isn't technically a sexual sound, it sends a shiver through me.

"You're the best, pretty girl," he murmurs.

"Don't you forget it," I say brightly, and Dante chuckles.

I continue to wash him, stroking my hand down his back, his chest, being careful to pat around his wound instead of wiping the cloth against it.

Dante hisses in a breath when I do so, but it doesn't seem to hurt him too much and I have to get the blood off.

"Be still," I scold, and he stops moving.

"Never thought a bullet through and through would hurt this fucking much," he says through gritted teeth.

"As opposed to what?"

Dante taps his right thigh. I see that there's a round, white scar there. I've noticed it before, but didn't think much of it. All wiseguys have scars. My father has plenty that I've seen while we were in the pool. I grew up in the life, so nothing much surprises me, I guess.

"Jimmy Sawbones had to dig this one out and I thought for sure I was going to die," he chuckles. "I was only nineteen, and it took my father and two of his men to hold me down."

I bite my lip. I hate to hear about him being hurt, but at the same time, something about it titillates me. Dante's led an exciting life while I've mostly been squirrelled away in my father's mansion.

Dante quirks an eyebrow, smirking at me. "Does that turn you on, pretty girl? All my war stories?"

"A little," I admit, and then I move my hand down between his legs, groping him. Dante moans, looking into my eyes.

"Don't start what you can't finish," he rasps, and I sigh heavily.

We haven't been able to make love because of my ribs, and I'm growing increasingly sexually frustrated.

"I'm still too sore," I mourn, but I continue stroking him, looking down and watching the way he plumps in my hand. "But I can take care of you."

"You don't have to do that," Dante says, but he's already gasping, thrusting forward into my hand. It feels good, to have him want me so much, have him desperate for me. I start thinking of ways maybe we could work it out, which positions might be less painful, but Dante's arching his back, his knuckles turning white on the edges of the bathtub.

I lean forward to kiss him and he returns the kiss sloppily, hungrily, exploring my mouth with his tongue and groaning into my mouth when he spills all over the cloth and my hand.

"That was fast," I giggle, and Dante groans and laughs at the same time.

"It's been too long," he defends himself, and then gives me a hot look.

I clear my throat and look away, trying to calm myself down. My skin feels hot all over and I want more, want him to touch me, but I can't think of a way that won't hurt.

"I'll take it from here," Dante tells me. "You get ready for bed. You look tired."

I'm not so much tired as I am worked up, but I don't tell Dante that. I head into the bedroom and change into a silk nightie that he bought me. I used to always sleep in the nude, but since Dante and I have had to be celibate, that didn't seem fair to him, so he'd bought me the nightie at a local boutique. The silk feels cool and good against my skin, and I slide under the covers, my body temperature finally seeming to go down just a little.

Dante doesn't bother with clothes, just drying off in the doorway of the bedroom and then crawling into bed with me. I pout at him.

"That's not fair," I whine.

Dante smirks. "Don't worry, baby. Gonna take care of you, too. Want you to sit on my face."

My eyes widen. "Dante, won't that hurt your shoulder?"

That's the reason he hasn't gone down on me in a week is because of the positioning and that he might strain it.

"It'll be fine. Besides, I don't care. Want to taste you," he mumbles, and who am I to say no to my husband when he's lying naked in bed next to me?

I shift, sitting up on my knees on the bed and straddling his face, looking down into his eyes. Dante reaches up slowly and grabs on to my hips, lowering me down onto his tongue. The nightie covers his face so I huff and pull it off me, throwing it on the floor.

Dante's mouth is hot against my sex and I gasp when he dips his tongue into my entrance. I rock my hips forward, but slowly, so that I don't stretch too far and hurt my ribs.

Dante clamps on to my hips to get his tongue deeper

and then he sticks it out wide, letting me grind myself against his tongue. When I catch the right rhythm, I know that it isn't going to take long.

"Dante," I moan. "Dante, I'm so close."

He takes in a deep breath through his nostrils and moves his tongue along me as I continue to roll my hips. It's slow and agonizing because I can't move too fast without my ribs aching, and my orgasm builds up slowly in my belly, making me feel like I'm being pulled up on a rollercoaster.

It takes only a few more rocks of my hips and rolls of Dante's tongue before I'm coming, grabbing on to the head-board and crying out.

Dante laps at me hungrily even after I'm finished, and I'm overstimulated so I shudder as pleasure keeps rolling through my body. His hands finally loosen over my hips and I roll off him. He sucks in air, smiling at me, his face covered in my juices.

I blush, but then I see the blood trickling down his shoulder.

"Oh, no!" I cry out, running to the bathroom to get a bandage. When I return, Dante looks down at it and groans.

"Think I popped a stitch," he says irritably.

"Shit!" I curse. "Let me call Jimmy," I say, grabbing for my phone, but Dante takes hold of my wrist.

"You know how to sew, right?"

I stare at him. "Wh-what?" I stammer.

Dante shrugs. "You're my wife now, Mia. You're going to have to learn to do first aid."

"This isn't first aid!" I argue.

He laughs. "For people like us, it is."

I guess he's right. I've seen my mother patch up my father plenty of times, although I've never witnessed her putting a stitch in him.

"What do I do?" I ask.

"Just get a needle and thread," Dante says easily, as if he's not bleeding profusely. "It's just the one stitch, so you'll just have to pinch the skin together and push through."

"Won't that hurt you?" I ask.

Dante points at the bottle of painkillers Jimmy gave us which is sitting on the desk. "Just hand me a couple of those."

I do as he asks and he dry swallows them. My hands are trembling as I go to the closet to get the needle and thread, thinking about when he'd first been hurt. I take a few deep breaths and it calms me slightly.

When I return, Dante's sitting up with his back braced against the headboard, splashing the whiskey he keeps at his bedside on the wound and hissing.

I start to move toward him but Dante holds up a hand to stop me.

"You've got to sterilize the needle," he commands. "Take that lighter you use for the candles, just heat it up for a second."

I do as he says and my hands aren't shaking anymore, thank God.

I pause when Dante winces as I stick the needle into his skin, holding the sides together, but after a minute, I get the hang of it and tie off the thread like my mother taught me when I was young and we were making pillows and little blankets.

Dante looks at my handiwork. "Good job, baby," he praises, and I sigh in relief, plopping back down on the bed after putting away the needle and thread.

He's turned over on his good shoulder, looking at me fondly. "You're good at this," he says.

"Good at what?"

He leans forward and brushes his nose against mine before kissing me chastely on the mouth. "Being my wife."

My heart swells in my chest. God, I love him. I love him so much, even if he's not ready to say the same to me.

"I love you," I say, unable to help myself, and Dante puts an arm around my waist, being careful not to stretch his shoulder.

He doesn't answer me, like usual, but he nuzzles against my neck and that's almost good enough.

When I open my eyes the next morning, it's because Dante has opened the balcony door, sliding it open gently. I haven't been sleeping that well lately, since the kidnapping, so it wakes me instantly.

He's on the phone, and I shift and am about to call out to him when I hear what he's saying.

"I'm still going to kill the bastard," he says in a low tone. *Shit. He's still going after Vincenzo.*

21

DANTE

Leonardo calls me way too early in the damn morning, sounding like he's just gotten out of the strip club downtown. "What the hell is this I hear about you working with Lorenzo?" he snarls.

I stand up, looking over at Mia, who's still sleeping, but fitfully. My heart aches. She's not been sleeping well, having nightmares, ever since the kidnapping. It makes me wish I'd have killed the sonofabitch myself.

I slide open the balcony door quietly. "I'm still going to kill the bastard," I say in a quiet tone. "I'm just playing the long game, Leo."

"Real fucking long!" Leo cries. Leonardo had been close to my father, almost like a surrogate brother to me, like Nico, and we've always gotten along, but he's too impulsive. He wants what he wants now and not later, and that can be a problem with what we do.

I sigh, looking out over the grounds. The gardener needs to come and cut the grass again.

I know how Leo feels. I'd felt the same way, at first, when I went over to Luca's to deal with Vincenzo.

"Listen, working with him just makes him trust me more," I explain. "I don't want him to see it coming. The Lorenzos are a big famiglia, and what good will it do us if I get popped right after I take care of him?" I pause.

"First you marry his daughter," Leo mumbles. "Then you don't take care of him. Every second he lives is disrespectful to Uncle Enzo," Leo insists, breathing hard. He's probably drunk and pissed off, but that doesn't excuse this kind of behavior.

"Who do you think you're talking to?" I ask in a calm, even tone.

Leo pauses. "I'm just...I thought you were going to take care of it."

"I'm going to take care of it," I promise. "I'm going to cut off his fucking head. Is that what you want to hear, Leo?"

He pauses again, so long if I didn't hear him breathing, I would have thought he hung up. "Sorry, *cugino*," he mumbles.

"*Capo*, to you," I growl, and Leo goes quiet again. "Now ditch this phone, you asshole."

I hang up the phone, huffing out a breath, and when I turn, Mia's standing at the balcony door, her blue eyes wide.

I freeze for a second. Did she hear the whole thing? Does she know who we were discussing? I don't remember what I said, so what if she knows what I'm planning?

I slide open the door, frowning. "What's wrong, pretty girl?" I ask, reaching out to touch her auburn hair, which is mussed from sleep.

"Nightmare," she murmurs, pressing her face into my chest. She wouldn't act this way if she knew the truth about my plans, right? She'd be devastated. Screaming bloody murder at me.

And why do I care so much that she still comes to me. That I don't hurt her?

I know that I'm getting too close to Mia. I know that I have feelings for her, deep ones, and last night it was all I could do not to say that I love her back. But I have to keep myself at some kind of a distance. I know that she'll hate me after I kill her father, and the very idea of it makes my stomach churn. Unless... unless I can keep it secret from her, set someone else up to take the fall?

Gallo would have been the obvious choice, but now that obviously isn't going to work. If there was only a way to keep it from her. To keep her loving me.

Despite how hard I'm fighting it, I can't help myself from falling for her.

I draw her into my arms, kissing the crown of her head.

"It's going to be okay, Mia," I tell her softly, murmuring it into her hair.

She sniffles. "Do you have to go to work today?" she asks.

I nod slowly. I've got to oversee the cleanup crew at the dry-cleaning joint, make sure they don't have sticky fingers. Vincenzo had been too stupid to check in the dryers, where I keep a lot of the pre-laundered cash.

I guess he'd had other things on his mind, like kidnapping my wife.

I draw in a breath. "I wish I could stay with you, pretty girl, but Nico's taking the night off and Alberto needs to stay here with you," I explain. "I'll be back as soon as I can."

Mia clutches at me, looking up at me. "I could go with you," she suggests.

I frown. "No, baby. You can't."

"Dante, please," she pleads. "Don't go."

I look down at her, concerned. "What's going on with you?"

She shakes her head. "Nothing, I'm just...the nightmare," she mumbles. "It was really scary."

"I'm going to take care of that," I promise her, and Mia looks up at me, searching my face with wild eyes.

"Dante..." She hesitates, closes her eyes and takes a deep breath. Something is definitely up.

"Pretty girl, please talk to me."

"I... I need you to be safe, please. I need you with me because..." her voice fades for a few seconds.

"It's okay baby, just say it, whatever it is. I'll do my best to give you anything you need."

"You can't give me anything this time, Dante. This is all me." Another deep breath, eyes closed tightly shut and then a whisper. "I'm pregnant."

She might have breathed the words, but the strength of the message makes me stumble backwards from the shock, standing naked again out on the balcony. Mia follows me, having slipped on her nightie.

She's *what*?

"What are you talking about?" I ask, all the blood draining from my face. It's one thing to almost be in love with Luca Lorenzo's daughter, but to have his grandchild? That's a slap in my father's face.

"I didn't plan this," she starts, babbling quickly. "I didn't know until yesterday. I don't know what to do. I don't even know if you want kids. *Do* you want kids?"

I look down at her, swallowing hard, my head spinning.

I've never thought about kids. It was never my priority. Taking over my father's business is my priority. Avenging my parents' deaths is my priority.

But lately, my priorities have shifted, and hearing about

the pregnancy just seems to make things worse, prove how far I've strayed.

I can't answer her, something stuck in my throat, and so I move past her, grabbing the first pair of pants I find in the closet and pulling them on. I don't even know if the shirt matches, and usually I'm pretty fashionable, but today I don't care.

I just need to get out of here.

"Dante, what are you doing? Where are you going?" Mia asks, coming inside without even shutting the balcony door.

"I have to work," I mumble.

"We need to talk about this," she says firmly, but I won't even look at her. I can't look at her. I grab yesterday's jacket, and head to my car.

She runs after me all the way down the stairs, standing in front of my car when I get inside.

I look at her for a long moment while she stands in the garage with her palms on the hood, and then I back out, screeching out onto the road.

I don't even know where I'm going until I end up at Nico's apartment in the city. I ring the doorbell over and over for what seems like fifteen minutes before he answers in nothing but his boxers, a sour look on his face.

"*Capo?*" His eyes widen. "What's wrong? Who's hurt?" When I don't answer, his face shifts, goes blank. "Who's dead?"

I shake my head. "It's not that," I mumble, pushing past him into the apartment.

A blonde is perched on the couch arm, looking offended in a bra with panties that don't match, and when I walk in, she glares at me.

Nico takes her by the arm, pulls her up. "Time to go," he says in a low voice.

"What? You're not kicking me out of here!" she screeches.

Nico doesn't answer, just pushes her out the door and closes it, ignoring her when she bangs on it.

"Tell me what happened," Nico says, hitching up his boxer briefs and sitting down on the couch, rummaging around for a beer on the counter littered with what is probably mostly empty bottles.

"It's kind of the opposite of dead," I say, barking out a laugh. "Mia's pregnant."

It sounds surreal the second I say it, like I'm talking about somebody else. This can't be happening.

Nico's face goes blank again and he nods slowly. "She asked me to get her a test yesterday, when you went to her dad's."

"And you didn't tell me?" I sit down hard on his old recliner and it squeaks and groans.

Nico doesn't live like I do. His sister lives well enough with their mother, and he helps them out a lot and stays over sometimes, but he says he needs his own space to decompress and breathe sometimes. I can totally relate. Especially right now.

"Not my story to tell," Nico says quietly, and I rub a hand across my mouth.

"I don't know what I'm going to do. I married her to get close to Luca, and all that happened was that I ended up working with the bastard instead of against him and ended up...."

I pause, not knowing what I was going to say. Was I going to say that I'm in love with her?

Am I?

Nico doesn't pry, and for that, I'm grateful.

"So, it's done? Gallo?" Nico asks.

"It's done." I sigh, resting my back against the recliner.

"His whole crew or just the man himself?"

"Just him," I answer, knowing what Nico means. Usually, when you take out a Caputo, you have to take out the whole famiglia to keep backlash from happening. "But I can't leave Mia alone that long. Especially not now."

"Leo, Alberto, and I could take care of it," Nico suggests, but I shake my head.

"Absolutely not. I won't send my men into danger when I can't be there. Give me a little credit. Besides, Leo just called this morning, giving me shit about Lorenzo."

Nico rubs a hand across the back of his neck. "Yeah, he's been a pain in the ass about it," he admits.

"He was *my* father," I mumble, more than a little irritated at Leo's call, his disrespect.

"Leo feels like Enzo was his father, too. You know that, *capo,*" Nico reminds me.

"I know. I also know you did too," I sigh. "I get it. I feel stuck, like I'm just at a standstill. I hate it, too. He doesn't seem to understand that."

"I do," Nico assures me. He leans forward, resting his forearms on his thighs. "Do you think that we could take out Lorenzo in secret? Pin it on someone else?"

"That's what I was thinking," I say, this strange combination of excitement and guilt rising in me. I'm ready to get rid of Luca, but at the same time, I think about what a daddy's girl Mia is. I think about how devastated she will be, and it hurts my heart. "But I don't know," I say slowly. "We'll have to find someone to pin it on."

Nico scoffs. "There's about a hundred men you could

pin it on, Dante. Luca Lorenzo doesn't have a shortage of enemies."

When I just stay silent, Nico adds, "You've changed, *capo*. You were never the type of man to hesitate."

I clenched my jaw, grinding my teeth. Nico's right. I have been hesitating. I thought I was biding my time, but really, aren't I just procrastinating? And all because of Mia.

I need to focus on my goal. I'm right at the end.

"Set up a meet with Lorenzo," I order, and Nico grins. "He told me he does business alone. Tell him it's a business call, and I'll take him out at the dinner table."

"That's more like it."

22

MIA

I scream when Dante backs out, slamming my fist on the garage door as it closes. Alberto walks out to the garage with a quizzical look, but I wave him away.

I'm not hurt or in trouble. I'm just *mad*.

The most I can hope for is that Dante is too shaken up to go after Vincenzo now that I've told him about the baby, but his reaction leaves a bad taste in my mouth.

He'd been so pale, just staring at me and not speaking. Does he not want this baby?

I don't know, and I can't believe he just walked out on me, without even talking to me about it. I consoled myself by calling Marta. All I have to tell her is "I need you" and in fifteen minutes, she's at my door with a bottle of my favorite wine.

I groan inwardly as she heads to the kitchen, pouring us both a glass.

"I can't," I say softly.

Marta scoffs. "You drank a bottle of this a night when we were teens," she jokes. "You can have one glass."

"No, I really can't," I insist, frustration growing in me,

anger at Dante, stress about the nightmares and Vincenzo Gallo. Everything is piling up and I don't know how to release it.

Marta doesn't listen, just keeps pouring, and before I know what I'm doing, I knock the glass off the counter and it shatters on the floor, spilling red wine onto the white tile.

She jumps and blinks at me.

"Shit," I curse. "I'm sorry, Marta. It's just...there's a lot going on."

"I know, honey," she says, coming closer to me and hugging me, stepping over the shattered glass.

I sniffle, tears streaming down my face. "It isn't just about Vincenzo," I admit. "I'm pregnant. I'm pregnant and I don't know if Dante and I are okay—"

"Wait, wait, go back. You're *pregnant*."

I nod miserably and Marta's mouth drops open.

"Congratulations?" she says, but her voice is hesitant, and it strikes me as so funny I manage a laugh, wiping my eyes. "Oh, and congratulations about that other thing, too."

I look into her eyes, confused. "What other thing?"

She shrugs, looking sly. "You know. Vincenzo being missing."

It slowly dawns on me what she's saying. Vincenzo Gallo is already dead. I've been freaking out about Dante getting hurt going after him, and he's already gone.

Likely, he's gone "missing" because they haven't found a body, and the famiglias in this city have good cleaners, so there will probably be no trace of him.

Relief floods through my body.

Marisa comes into the kitchen, her brow furrowed. "What happened?" she asks, looking at me and Marta and the broken glass on the floor.

I smile sheepishly. "I'm just clumsy, Marisa, don't worry. I'll clean it up."

"Nonsense," she scoffs, going into the closet and grabbing the broom. She shoos Marta and me out of the kitchen and we go out by the pool, sitting on the edge with our feet in the water like we used to at my father's pool back when we were kids.

"I'm glad you're here," I say, leaning against her, and she rests her head on top of mine.

"I'll always be here for you, silly," she says.

"I've been so worried about Dante going after Vincenzo," I groan. "And all this time it was already done."

"If it makes you feel any better, I heard your father had a hand in it," Marta says conspiratorially.

I smile. I'm sure he did. My father is even more protective than Dante, and that's saying something.

"I'm just glad he's gone," I admit. I wish the nightmares would be gone right along with him, but something tells me they'll hang around.

"How have you been?" Marta asks, and I shrug.

"Good and bad," I explain. "Dante and I are doing pretty well, but he still hasn't said it."

"That he loves you?" Marta raises an eyebrow.

I nod, feeling oddly embarrassed. Most people aren't married to a man who won't say "I love you," are they?

Marta hums. "You just have to give him time. Especially now that you're pregnant. He's probably freaking out."

"Probably," I agree, laughing a little. "The look on his face..."

I lose my smile. The way he'd acted – does it mean that he doesn't want the baby? What will I do? I guess I'll have to move out, move back in with my father. The thought of it makes my heart ache, makes my stomach churn.

Marta pats my knee. "Stop worrying so much. I see it all over your face," she scolds.

I give her a weak smile. "I'll try."

Marta and I change into swimsuits and do a few laps, splashing at each other in the pool like kids. I needed this time with her, time to decompress and not feel dread and stress at every moment.

I feel tired after we get out of the pool, but in a good way, like I've had a good workout. My muscles feel loose instead of tense for the first time in weeks. Stress isn't good for the baby, so maybe I should do things like this more often.

After Marta leaves to go home, I lie on the couch, scrolling through my phone, looking at cribs and changing tables. There seems to be so many things to put in the nursery. I wonder, idly, if it's a boy or a girl and feel a rush of love for my unborn child. I never imagined I would feel maternal this early in my pregnancy, but just the idea of a baby makes me feel happy.

I just wish that Dante felt the same way.

I'm still angry at him, and it just gets worse as I wait and wait for him to get home. It's nearing dusk when he finally walks in, and I promptly get up and stalk up to the bedroom, slamming the door and locking it.

Dante tries the knob and then knocks on the door. "Mia," he calls. "Let me in."

"Absolutely not," I say through the door, huffing out a breath. "You walked out on me, Dante."

"I know," he said, sounding chagrined. "And I'm sorry. I was just surprised. Can we...can we talk about this? About what you want to do about the baby?"

My mouth drops open. What does he mean, what do *I*

want to do? I unlock the door and jerk it open, glaring at him.

"What do you mean, what do *I* want to do? I want to have our baby, Dante. I love it just as much as I love you already. I've told you a million times how much I love you, even though you never say it back!" My voice raises and trembles.

He sets his jaw, staring back at me intensely, his hazel eyes flashing. He runs a hand through his hair, letting out a frustrated breath.

"If you want this baby, I do too," he says quietly, and it's so unlike what I thought he would say that I'm taken aback, blinking at him. "I've never thought about having kids, but if it makes you happy, then I'm happy."

I stare at him, wary. "Are you just telling me what you think I want to hear?"

Dante takes my hand and I don't pull away. "Can I show you something?"

I follow him as he leads me down the stairs and into the garage. He opens the trunk of his car and inside is a big box containing a crib.

"I thought we'd need one of these," he says quietly, and tears well in my eyes. I throw my arms around him, hugging him tightly, and Dante's arms go around my waist.

I bury my face in his chest, feeling a myriad of emotions swirl through me. It's like everything has finally calmed down and I can breathe again, and I cry into his shirt for a few moments before pulling away.

He leans down to kiss me, softly, but I deepen the kiss and it's intimate and sweet and unlike any other time we've kissed before.

Does he love me? I feel like I can sense it, like I can feel it through his kiss like osmosis, but I need to hear it. I need to hear him say it.

"Do you love me, Dante?" I ask softly against his mouth, and Dante stiffens.

He pulls away, looking down into my eyes.

"Of course I do, pretty girl," he says softly, brushing a strand of hair away from my face. "Didn't I risk my life to save you? Twice?" He chuckles.

I search his face, looking to try and guess if he's lying. It's still not the same as hearing those three little words that would mean so much to me, but it's better than nothing.

I'll take anything I can get when it comes to Dante Ricci.

23

DANTE

I don't sleep that night, thinking about the baby and what I'm planning to do to my wife's father. The meeting with Luca is at dinner, and I hope he's alone, because I don't like my work getting messier than it has to.

Mia and I spend the day setting up the crib in the bedroom right next to the master bedroom, which we've decided is the best place for the nursery. I still can't wrap my head around it, her being pregnant. She's going to have my baby, and I have no idea how to feel about it.

This is more serious than just marrying her to get close to her father. Hell, this is even more serious than possibly falling in love with her. But I have to make her happy. Worse, I *want* to make her happy, and I'm so conflicted I just try not to think too much, try to enjoy spending time with her.

"I have a meeting tonight," I tell her, not wanting her to be surprised or try and keep me from going. I know that she gets anxious when I'm working, and it's understandable, given everything that happened.

Mia nods idly, not having much of a reaction, and I'm

happy. Hopefully, things are calming down. Although they're about to get a lot more stressful for her. Guilt rockets through me and I put my arms around her waist, hugging her from behind and kissing along the side of her face.

She giggles and leans back against me. "Hurry back. Marisa says she's making dinner."

I hum in the back of my throat and kiss her cheek again before reluctantly letting her go. "It shouldn't take too long."

The words feel like acid in my mouth because I know that I'm going to be changing her life forever in just a few hours.

I do my best to keep my mind blank as I drive to Luca's, leaving Nico in charge of guarding the house and Mia. He asks me three times if I need backup.

"No," I say firmly. "I need to do this on my own."

It's my mission, this revenge. It's the only thing I've been thinking about since my father died, and I thought I'd be happy, but instead I just feel numb.

Mia and my feelings for her have complicated everything.

I ring the doorbell and expect Luca to come to the door, just like before, but instead, it's a petite blonde with striking blue eyes. It only takes me a second to realize they're the same shade as Mia's.

"Hello," she says in a heavily accented voice. "You must be my son-in-law."

She smiles brightly, and I can see Mia all over her features.

I swallow hard. I hadn't been expecting this. Luca said he always does business alone.

"Yes," I say awkwardly, and hold out my hand for her to shake.

She chuckles and pulls me into a brief hug before pulling away, still smiling.

"I'm Anastasia," she says. "It's lovely to meet you. Luca's in the kitchen. Come, I've made stroganoff."

It smells delicious in the dining room and Anastasia pulls out a seat for me. I sit, clearing my throat. What the hell am I going to do now? I have no reason to kill Mia's mother, and it seems like an awful thing to do since I'm going to be killing her father, too. I don't want that.

Luca comes into the kitchen, setting the table. At least he's sent the staff away, and I don't have to worry about that. I'll figure this out. This is my chance, and I'm not going to miss it, no matter how conflicted I feel.

"Will you be joining us for dinner?" I ask Mia's mother, and the blonde smiles.

Luca finishes setting the table and he puts an arm around his wife, kissing her temple.

"She'll be going to her sister's," Luca says. "Anastasia doesn't like listening in on business."

"I wanted to meet you," she explains.

"It's lovely to meet you," I say, doing my best to sound charming and smiling at her.

Anastasia looks at me, something wary in her gaze. "I hope you enjoy dinner, Dante."

She leaves quietly and I feel slightly exposed and I don't know why. There's something suspicious about the way Mia's mother looked at me, and the feeling that something is off makes me wonder if I should abandon the plan for today.

But then I watch Luca kiss his wife tenderly goodbye, and I think about how my father will never get to do that to Marisa again. How many years he missed out on doing that with my mom. I think about how he'll never meet his grandchild, and it strengthens my resolve. I'm going to do this. I have to do this.

When Luca walks Anastasia to the door, I take my gun out of the back of my pants, cocking it, covering the sound with a cough, and resting it in my lap.

Luca returns and sits at the head of the table a few feet away. It's close enough range that I can't miss. Something in me wants him to admit it, wants him to confess, so I want to engage him in conversation.

"Your wife is very beautiful," I comment, taking a bite of the stroganoff. It's rich and heady on my tongue.

"Thank you," Luca says, smiling.

"You seem to be very happy together."

"We weren't always," he admits, chuckling.

I raise an eyebrow. "Why's that?"

Luca shrugs. "I was young and stupid when we got married. I wanted a wife but just to say that I had one, you know? I wanted to put her on some kind of shelf and forget about her when I had my fun."

"So, you cheated on her?" I ask point-blank.

Luca sighs. "I did."

"Was it a mistake?"

"Every single time," he says quietly. "I lost sight of what was important, didn't make the right decisions. I got wrapped up in work and the lifestyle and forgot that there was real life to be lived. Real love to be felt."

"What changed?" I ask curiously. I've never heard a wiseguy say that a mistress was a mistake. It seems like it's a common thread in our lifestyle, and even though I'd never consider it, it's surprising to hear Luca talking this way.

"Mia," Luca says with a bright smile. "She was born and I didn't know what the hell I was doing. I stayed out all night almost every night, avoided her like the plague. I threw myself into work and women and Anastasia was alone all the time. But then one night, I came home from work and Mia's walking around. I didn't even know she *could* walk. She toddles over to me and takes my thumb in her hand, looking up at me with those big blue eyes just like her mother's." Luca's smile is warm, his eyes dreamy and nostalgic.

He really does love Mia. Guilt washes through me once again, but I push it out of my mind, slowly putting my gun in my hand and pointing it at him under the table. This is the time to do it, while he's distracted, while he's reminiscing.

"That was the moment I decided," Luca says.

"Decided what?" I ask, and I don't know why I'm asking. I should just do it. I should just pull the trigger, but something's stopping me.

"I decided to choose life over death. Love over hate."

I look at him for a long moment, my hand tight on the handle of my gun. I think of Mia, the way her face will crumple when she hears the news, the stress she'll be under while she's newly pregnant. I think about choosing life over death, choosing love over hate.

I'm stuck, pointing the gun but not shooting it, and Luca shifts at the table.

"Excuse me for a moment. I forgot the wine," he says, and stands up to go back into the kitchen.

I let out a long breath and put my gun back in the holster at my spine.

Luca returns with the wine and I wait for a few moments before taking my phone out of my pocket and frowning down at it.

"I'm sorry to cut this short, but I have to go," I say, and Luca waves his hand dismissively.

"I know how it goes." He looks at me for a long moment. "What was the business you wanted to talk to me about?"

I don't miss a beat. "The Gallos," I say. "We're finishing that up, yeah?"

Luca nods. "Within the week," he promises.

"Good," I say. "Thank Anastasia for dinner."

"Ask Mia to call her," Luca says. "She's been worried about her."

I nod tersely and leave as quickly as I can.

My head is spinning and all I want is to get home to Mia. When I arrive, she's asleep on the couch, her phone in her hand as if she was waiting for me to call. My heart clenches in my chest and I kneel down next to her, kissing her forehead.

"Mia," I call, and she mumbles and shifts, rolling over. Her dark eyelashes fan across her cheekbones. I don't want to wake her. She looks so peaceful, and she sleeps so little lately.

I pick her up gingerly, bridal style, and she tucks her head against my chest, not waking.

She still doesn't wake when I place her in bed, not even bothering to undress her or myself before crawling into bed with her and pulling up the duvet around us. I hold her tighter than I ever have before, and she sighs in contentment.

I think I'm in love with Mia Lorenzo, but I don't know how to stop wanting to avenge my parents' death. The fact that I'd choked when I had the chance to kill Luca shocks me. I'm shaken, and I don't know where to go from here.

I've never felt so lost, never felt so torn, but with Mia in my arms, I'm able to push it all away, and it's like she's the only person in the world. With her safe in my arms, I'm able to drift off to sleep.

24

MIA

A couple of days pass, and Dante has to work most of the time, coming home tired and going straight to bed after dinner. I don't mind it as much now that I know that Vincenzo is out of the picture, and because Dante had confirmed that he loves me.

I spend my time in the nursery, painting it a pretty green so that it'll fit for either a boy or a girl. Dante has already set up the crib, and I'm just waiting for the changing table to get here. It's coming together nicely, and I can just imagine my baby in the crib, looking up at the mobile that I've ordered.

Dante yawns, standing at the door of the nursery, just in a pair of sweats. He's not dressed for the day, which is unusual. He comes up behind me, putting his arms around me and kissing the back of my neck.

"I'm sorry I slept in," he murmurs, and I turn to him, smiling.

"It's okay. I've got plenty to do today if you've got work. They're delivering the changing table and I wanted to paint the trim."

"We can hire someone to do the painting, you know?" Dante says, and I scoff.

"I want to do it myself. Our baby will be sleeping here. I want it to have a mother's touch."

Dante smiles down at me and kisses me on the bridge of my nose, his arms still loosely around my waist. "I actually thought I'd stay in today, get some rest."

My eyes widen. "Dante Ricci? Willingly getting rest?"

He snorts. "I know, it's a miracle. You're welcome to lie in bed with me if you want, but I thought I'd give you some cash to get your hair and nails done."

I gasp, excited. With all the commotion that has happened so far in our marriage, I've let myself go just a bit when it comes to my appearance. I've lost too much weight and my auburn hair has been looking dull without my usual highlights.

"Really?" I ask, and Dante hugs me to him.

"Of course, pretty girl. Why don't you go out and have a girl's day?"

"I could call Marta," I muse, and look up at him, smiling mischievously. "But then I'd need more money."

Dante grins. "You drive a hard bargain, but you got it, baby."

I squeal excitedly, hugging him and going to get dressed in a simple T-shirt and jeans with open toed shoes so I can get a pedicure, too.

Dante enters the bedroom while I'm sliding on my shoes to hand me a stack of cash that I put into my purse, kissing him quickly.

"When you come back, we'll have dinner, yeah?" he suggests, and I beam at him.

"Thank you, baby."

Dante pats me on the butt as I head for the stairs, and I

giggle, calling Marta. She agrees to meet me at the hair salon.

I'm humming while they file my nails and Marta stares at me curiously.

"You're certainly in a good mood compared to last time," she says.

"Dante's just been wonderful," I gush.

"I'm so happy for you," Marta says dryly, and I can't help but laugh a little. Her dad still hasn't accepted that she loves Rocco. "No, but really, I am," she assures me.

"I know you are."

"Did you finally have the talk about the baby?" she gestures down to my still-flat stomach.

"We did. He told me he was shocked at first but then he bought a crib, told me that if I was happy, he was happy. He told me he loves me," I say with a huge grin.

Marta raises an eyebrow. "He said that?"

I deflate, but only a little. I'm having a good day and I won't let my negative thoughts ruin this for me. "Not in so many words, but he answered yes to my question. That's enough, isn't it?"

"If it's enough for you, it's enough for me," she says, but then she keeps talking about it. "I wonder what his hangup is. You think it's a bad breakup or something?"

My shoulders slump and I lose my smile. I think about Felicia Nunez and how she'd showed up at our house. Surely she wouldn't have done that if it was really just a fling like Dante and Nico thought.

"You think it was Felicia?" I ask, unable to help myself.

Marta snorts. "That bimbo? Absolutely not."

I giggle at Marta's disdain and we turn our conversation to less serious matters, like how she has to sneak around at all hours to be with Rocco.

But thoughts about Dante and Felicia and their possible intense, emotional relationship keep trying to creep back into my mind. I want to trust that what Dante tells me is true, but the way I grew up...

My father was barely home until I was four or five years old, and all I remember from that time is Mama crying every night. I found out later that my father had mistresses – more than one of them. My mother assures me that all of that changed by the time I began school, but still, I think about it a lot and it clearly affects my relationships.

I blankly stare out into space and Marta nudges my shoulder as we sit at the hair dryers.

"You're still thinking about Dante and Felicia, aren't you?"

I groan. "I can't help it! You know how it is with our fathers."

I know that Marta went through the same thing with her mother and father.

"But it's different for you," Marta points out. "Your father changed."

"You're right," I say, sighing.

"Dante could change, too," Marta suggests, and I nod, thinking about it.

Maybe Dante *has* changed. Maybe I'm worried for no reason, just like I was about Vincenzo. Am I creating problems for myself when they really aren't there?

"He hasn't shown any signs of cheating so far, has he?"

I shake my head. "I was worried when we first got married." I grimace. "Like when Felicia showed up to our house. But nothing like that has happened since."

Marta shrugs. "Then maybe it's not a problem. You might be making a fuss over nothing."

"Probably," I mutter. "I'm good at that."

She laughs. "We're all guilty of it from time to time." She pats my shoulder. "Oh, how are your ribs doing?"

"I'm not even wearing the wrap anymore," I say proudly. "It doesn't hurt hardly at all."

"That's wonderful." Marta pauses and gives me a sly grin. "So, does that mean your...bedroom activities are back in full swing?"

I frown. "Not exactly. Dante's been working so much."

Marta sighs. "That's the life, I guess."

"It is," I agree. It's a theme in my life, all the men I love working constantly. I know that they do it to keep us in nice things, to keep us protected, but it can still be lonely, being a woman in the famiglia.

But things have been going well as they can be, especially given the added stress of what happened to me and the baby. Dante's been handling it better than I expected, actually, and he doesn't seem to be seeking anything outside our marriage.

I'm lucky, really. There are women who have to grit their teeth and bear it when their husbands go out to see their mistresses. Dante is faithful and he's been attentive ever since he found out about the baby.

"You're a lucky girl," Marta says, as if reading my mind, and I give her a big smile.

"I am," I say, humming and looking down at my painted toes.

I've always been a bit spoiled, I can admit that, and Dante spoils me all the same as my father did. They're a lot alike, really, and I think idly that I should plan a family dinner for all four of us and tell them about the baby.

My parents will be thrilled.

"I still can't believe you're pregnant," Marta says incredulously. "Do you have a feeling if it's a boy or a girl? My mother says that with my brother, she was convinced it was a boy from the moment she figured out she was pregnant. I'm skeptical."

I snort. "You should be skeptical, because I have literally no idea," I admit. "Besides, it's just a little peanut right now. I have a doctor's appointment on Monday to see how far along I am."

Marta bounces excitedly. "Make sure you get pictures and send them to me."

I smile, grateful for Marta's continued support. "Of course I will. I still have to tell my parents."

She chuckles. "That kid is going to have your dad wrapped around their little finger."

I smile, thinking of my father holding a baby, cooing down at it. He loves babies and kids, always has, and I've seen him with lots of my cousins.

I can't wait to have him meet my child.

And I can't wait to get home to Dante and my perfect, happy life.

Marta's right. I am a lucky girl.

25

DANTE

The day off I spend does wonders for my mood, and when Mia comes home, I've got dinner set out on the table for her.

"Oh my God," she says, dropping her purse in the dining room. "It smells so good, Dante."

"Thank you," I murmur. "It's my mother's recipe. Eggplant parmigiana."

Mia puts her arms around me, squeezing me tight and kissing me quickly across the lips. "I'm so lucky," she says against my mouth, and I chuckle.

"Taste it before you say that."

She laughs and sits down at the table. I sit across from her and push a glass of sparkling cider toward her.

"I know it isn't wine," I say apologetically, "but it was the best I could do."

Mia looks at me, her blue eyes shining. "You really pamper me, Dante."

I smile. "I do my best."

I don't tell her that I've never spoiled a woman before, that I'm not the type to do these kinds of thoughtful, romantic things. Something about her brings it out of me.

Either that, or I just feel so guilty about what I almost did to her father a few days ago that I want to make up for it.

I still haven't decided how I'm going to go about exacting my revenge, but I haven't given it up, yet. I can't. I think about my father and rage boils in me that's directed all at Luca Lorenzo.

"Was the changing table delivered today?" she asks.

I shake my head. "Not yet."

She frowns and I laugh, beginning to eat.

"You know we have quite a few months before the nursery needs to be ready," I tease her.

"I know, but I want everything to be ready for the baby," she pouts. "It's good to be prepared."

She begins to eat, moaning at the taste. "Dante, this is so good."

I quirk an eyebrow, heat pooling in my lower stomach. "Hey, you're supposed to save those sounds for me," I say in a low tone, and Mia gives me a hot look.

"After all this, you're definitely going to get lucky," Mia croons, and I grin.

It's been too many days since we last made love. Mia looks at me curiously.

"Is that why you did all this? To get lucky?" she jokes.

I shrug. "I mean, it's definitely a bonus," I admit. "But I just wanted to do something nice for you. You've been so stressed, and now with the baby...stress isn't good for a pregnancy."

Mia's lip trembles. "You're so sweet, Dante."

I look away, embarrassed. "I just want you to be happy," I say honestly.

I compliment Mia on her hair and nails and she tells me all about Marta's drama with her wiseguy lover, which isn't really my idea of a fun dinner conversation, but it seems to amuse her. I just watch her talk for a moment, the way she's animated with her hands, the way her blue eyes sparkle, and my chest feels warm.

I do feel something for her. It's something strong, and real, and something I've never felt for anyone before. But I can't say that I love her. Not when I'm plotting to kill her father.

"Let's go out onto the terrace," I say after we finish up dinner. "Marisa will clean up tomorrow."

Mia agrees and I lead her out. She braces her hands on the railing of the terrace and looks out over the grounds. I put my arms around her, placing my hands on top of hers. Mia sighs and leans back against me.

I point up at the stars. "That's Orion's belt," I point out. "And the big dipper is over there. See if you can find the little dipper."

Mia looks up at the stars and I slide my hands on the waistband of her jeans, unbuckling them. Mia gasps.

"Dante," she calls, but her tone isn't scolding, more sensual.

"It's not like anyone will see us," I murmur. Nico and Alberto aren't here because I've stayed home today, and it's too late for the gardener to be here. Marisa's upstairs, sound asleep.

Mia hums happily and helps me pull off her jeans. I look down at her ass, grabbing it with both hands and watching as it jiggles.

Mia moans and leans over the railing, spreading her thighs and my mouth goes dry. I push down the sweats I've been wearing all day and press into her slowly as she leans forward further over the railing.

It's exhilarating, making love outside under the stars,

and my breath hitches in my chest as she clenches around me, getting used to me.

"You're so tight, pretty girl," I moan, and she pushes back against me and I almost see stars.

"All yours," she murmurs, and I thrust forward almost involuntarily. She grasps on to the railing, crying out my name.

"I was going to take this slow," I comment. "I was going to make you come over and over, but I don't think I can help myself."

My balls ache and I want to spill inside her, but I grit my teeth, holding back and trying to make my movements slow and steady. I don't want to hurt her ribs.

"Faster, Dante," Mia whimpers. "Harder, please."

My hips thrust forward but then I stop, frowning. "But your ribs—"

"They're nearly healed, please," she pleads, and that's all I need.

I fuck her hard and fast and she jolts forward, bracing herself on the railing. The cool air feels good on my hot skin as I pump in and out of her.

"I'm so close," she mumbles, turning back to look at me with her blue eyes glassy with lust.

I grunt and reach around her body to press my thumb against her clit, and she draws in a sharp breath, pushing back against me.

I don't think about the rhythm anymore, don't think about taking it slow, just chasing my orgasm.

"I'm close," I growl, and Mia whines out a long moan.

"I'm coming, Dante, don't stop!"

I listen to her words, listen to her body and thrust harder and faster into her until she's pulsing around me, wet and slick and hot.

I spill inside her just a few thrusts later, my shoulder still aching slightly but not nearly as bad as it would have been a week ago.

"Fuck," I curse, and Mia giggles and then moans as I slowly pull out of her.

"It's been too long," she comments, and she wiggles completely out of her jeans and pulls off her top, discarding her clothes on the terrace floor.

I grin at her, appreciating her naked body.

"Let's go for a swim," she suggests, wrapping her arms around my neck and kissing me hard and hungry.

It's a wonderful idea and the heated pool feels good on my injured shoulder. She splashes and plays like a kid and my heart skips a beat every time she smiles at me.

She swims over toward me, wraps her arms and legs around me as I stand up around the five foot mark.

I look at her, swallowing hard, feeling suddenly vulnerable because I want to tell her. I want to tell her that I love her, that no one else makes me feel this way, that no one ever has.

"Mia," I start.

"Shh," she quiets me with a kiss, deep and searching. We kiss for a long time in the water, so long that my hands and feet begin to prune.

We pad back to the bedroom, still wet from the pool, and I begin to run the shower while she pouts into the mirror.

"I ruined my hairstyle," she complains, and I can't help but laugh.

"You can get it fixed tomorrow," I assure her, and Mia climbs into the shower first, beckoning me with one hand.

I get in under the warm spray and I think about what a wonderful day this has been, taking time off work, spending it with Mia. Is this what choosing life over death is? Love over hate?

It feels better than the never-ending rage of vengeance. It feels better than the ache of grief, the sting of hatred. It feels like I'm home for the first time since my father died, here with her, and I wish I had the words to tell her that.

I can't tell her any of it. I can't tell her anything, so instead I kiss her, again and again until she's moaning into my mouth.

Then I kneel and put one of her legs over my shoulder, pressing my face into her sex, kissing her clit over and over until it's swollen and she's got her fingers in my hair, pressing me into her. I slide two fingers inside her as I lap at her and she comes almost immediately, grinding her hips against my face.

"Thank you for today," she says after we climb into bed together, after all our limbs are entangled.

I can't find my voice so I just kiss along her throat, make a mark on her neck, kissing and sucking there before I pull away to look at it. I'm satisfied with the purple mark and I kiss her mouth.

She hums in contentment and turns toward me, putting both her arms around my waist.

"I love you, Dante," she says, and my throat aches with how badly I want to say it back.

My chest aches with how much I want to tell her that she's home to me.

"Goodnight, pretty girl," is all I manage to say, and she's asleep for a long time before I finally drift off.

I wake up to an ear-splitting scream, and my heart leaps up into my throat. Mia bolts upright next to me, her chest heaving, and I put my arms around her. She fights me at first but then relaxes against me, sobbing into my chest. Rage boils in me toward a dead man, toward Vincenzo Gallo, because I know she's had another nightmare. It's been weeks since she's had one, and I wish I could bring him back to life just to kill him all over again.

"I dreamed about the warehouse again," Mia whimpers, shuddering in my arms. "I dreamed that you didn't make it, that you were lying on the floor, blood pooling all around you." She chokes out a sob, clutching at me.

"That didn't happen," I assure her. "I'm okay. We're both okay."

"But what if one day you're not?" she asks, gasping in air. "What if you get killed and I'm left all alone with this baby?'

"I'll never leave you alone," I say fiercely, and as I say it, I realize that I mean it. I won't leave her, even if I do end up killing her father. I'll have to keep that secret for the rest of my life, and it may send me to an early grave, but I can't let her go.

It takes Mia half an hour to fall asleep again, cuddled in my arms, and I think that before I do anything to Luca, I may need his help to take out every branch on the Gallo family tree.

Tomorrow, I may just do it myself.

26

MIA

I wake up to an empty bed and frown when I reach out for Dante and he's not there. I pad to the bathroom and look at myself in the mirror.

My hair isn't exactly ruined from the pool since it's salt water, but it's certainly not as luxurious as it was yesterday, and my eyes are puffy from crying.

I hate that I ruined my lovely night with Dante with another nightmare, and I want to apologize to him. I get dressed and walk out into the hallway and hear low voices coming from down the stairs.

I hear Nico's voice first, and I freeze.

"*Capo* wants us to finish it off, cut the tree down," he says, and instantly I know what he's talking about. It's about taking out the rest of the Gallos to keep them from retaliating. My breath comes shorter and I think for an awful moment that I'm going to have a panic attack, but I breathe in through my nose, out through my mouth, until I calm myself.

Dante comes out of the nursery, smiling, and I have to pretend I don't know anything is wrong. I plaster on a smile.

"The changing table came," he says happily, leading me into the nursery, and my heart is still beating too fast as I see where he placed it, right beneath the window.

"Thanks for setting it up," I mumble, still feeling so anxious I can barely stand it.

"Of course." Dante kisses my temple and then begins to massage my shoulders. "Are you feeling all right? You feel so stiff?"

"Just the bad dream, I guess," I lie, knowing that I'm not supposed to be listening in on his men. I don't want to make him angry, but at the same time, I don't want him to go off and get hurt. Any member of the Gallos could get off a stray bullet and... I can't even think about it.

I turn and wrap my arms around him, leaning up to kiss him hungrily, and Dante returns the kiss, but when I make it more aggressive, sliding my tongue into his mouth, he groans and pulls away, smiling.

"I've got too much work to do today to be late," he scolds me gently, and my heart begins to race again.

He's already dressed, all ready to go out and get this done, and I don't want him to go. I want him home safe with me. I know that it's irrational, expecting a wiseguy to stay home safe with me all the time, but I can't help it.

"Stay with me," I plead. "One more day."

"I can't, pretty girl," he murmurs, and hugs me tight before walking back out into the hallway. I follow him, desperate.

"Can I go with you?" I ask, and he turns to me, frowning, pausing at the top of the stairs.

"Of course not, Mia. I wouldn't let you come even if you weren't pregnant, but..."

I bite my lip. "Is Nico going to be with me?"

Dante shakes his head. "Marisa's downstairs making breakfast. She'll call if anything happens," he says.

"I don't feel safe," I say suddenly, knowing that he'll respond to that, and Dante sighs.

"I need Nico for the job, but Alberto can stay here with you, just to be safe."

I take a deep breath, realizing that I'm not going to win this. Dante isn't going to put off an important job just because I'm afraid that he'll get hurt. It's not realistic for me to expect that.

"Thank you," I say finally, getting myself together. "You take such good care of me."

Something flashes across Dante's face, something I can't quite put my finger on, and he turns his hazel eyes away from me.

"I'll see you soon," he mumbles, and kisses me quickly on the lips.

I stay at the top of the stairs until I hear Dante and Nico leave, and then take another a deep breath and descend the stairs.

Marisa indeed does have breakfast on the table, and my stomach rumbles. I've had morning sickness for a while, but I'm also always ravenously hungry. It's a bit of a conundrum, and now that I feel anxious about Dante getting hurt, my stomach rolls.

"Biscuits first," Marisa orders as I sit down. "It'll calm your stomach before the meat."

I smile at her. She's a kind, maternal woman and she keeps to herself most of the time, but it's obvious that she cares about me, and especially Dante.

I munch on the biscuits and she's right, it does seem to stop my stomach from churning. I wonder briefly how Marisa knew that would work.

"Do you have children?" I ask her, and Marisa looks at me, giving me a slightly sad smile.

She shakes her head. "I'm unable to have them. But Dante is close enough to my own son."

I nod, understanding. "What was he like as a kid?" I ask, curious now that we're having one of our own.

Marisa chuckles. "He was a little pain in my neck, that one. Always getting into trouble. He wanted to be a wiseguy from the moment he was born. Ran after his father all day long, and once, he snuck out with him on a job."

My eyes widen, thinking of how horribly dangerous that is. "What happened?"

"Enzo caught him halfway there and scolded him, sent him back to the house. He came to me with a big sigh. He was about twelve, thirteen. He said 'Marisa, I'm going to be the toughest guy in town. Just like Papa.'" She smiles, looking nostalgic.

I laugh. "I guess he followed his dreams, then."

She gives me a shrewd look. "Don't let Dante fool you. He's tough, sure, but he has the biggest heart of anyone I know." She pauses. "He'll do anything to protect the ones he loves. Just like Enzo."

She sighs, looking sad for a moment before she pushes a plate of Italian sausage at me. "Now, the meat. Protein is good for the baby."

The rest of the day goes by as slow as molasses as I wait to hear something, anything, from Dante. I notice Alberto checking his phone.

"Is everything okay?" I ask, and he nods his head easily, smiling at me.

Alberto's a sweet guy, even if he can't communicate that well. He carries around a pen and paper usually, and he scribbles something down for me.

I squint at the paper. *Everything's fine,* it reads.

But there's something on his face that makes me suspicious. I've been around the famiglia for a long time, and I consider myself pretty good at reading people who don't like to be read.

So, when Alberto gets up to use the bathroom, I sneak over to look at his phone. It's locked, but there's a text notification that I can read.

We're putting off breaking the hourglass.

I stare at it for a long time, swallowing hard. Wiseguys speak in code, and I'm pretty well-versed in deciphering it after a lifetime as my father's daughter.

It takes me a moment, though, because it's just such a shock to my system.

The hourglass is my father's insignia. He's used it since he was a kid, has a tattoo of it on his right shoulder blade, a tipped over hourglass with sand pouring out of it.

When I asked him about it as a kid, he'd chuckled.

"It reminds me, carissima," he told me.

"Reminds you of what, Papa?" I'd asked, fascinated as we sat on the edge of the pool, looking at the ink etched into his skin.

"Reminds me that time is always running out."

Time is certainly running out for him now. My husband is on a mission to kill my father.

27

DANTE

Leo's bouncing around in the backseat while Nico drives, humming. They're both happy to be out of the house, happy to be doing this job.

"This is just a rehearsal for the real show," Leo says.

It feels like there's a knot in my throat. Leo's been on my ass to get the job done when it comes to Luca, and I know that I've had chances to do it that I haven't taken. I still curse to myself when I think about how close I came the other day at dinner. I can't seem to get myself to do it, worried about Mia.

But there's no way I'm going to tell Leo that.

"Should be fun," Nico comments. "It's been a while." He cracks his knuckles as we pull up a half a mile from the Gallo mansion. Rumor has it that Vincenzo's brother, Romeo, is out for my blood, and I'm not about to allow them to take a shot at me.

He's taken over for Vincenzo since he's gone missing. They're so sure that it's me that they're not targeting Luca, which is good because if Luca goes, I want to be the one to kill him. No matter what's going on with my feelings for

Mia, I still dream about looking him in the face, getting him to admit he killed my father.

I missed my chance before, but I won't do that again.

We all exit the car and Nico pops the trunk. Leo nearly dives into it, excited to get to the weapons. He takes out a rifle and a bowie knife while Nico picks out just a handgun. I've got my gun in my spine holster and I pick up another handgun, just to be safe, and a pocketful of ammo.

"There's likely at least five of them in the house, all Gallo blood. Then there'll be guards outside," Nico explains.

"I don't care if there's a hundred of them," Leo says, cocking his rifle.

"Don't go in half-cocked," I warn dryly. Leo has zero impulse control and he's likely to get us all killed. "We're going to do this right, and quiet."

Leo nods, looking sheepish.

We walk the perimeter and we make it all the way to the yard before Nico pauses.

"Something smells here," he says, grimacing. "We should have come across a guard by now."

"Do you think they're ready for us?" Leo asks.

Nico tilts his head. "I don't know. All I know is that something's not right."

We sneak around the back of the grounds, sticking close to the trees in case we have to duck behind one, and walk up slowly to mansion.

"Fuck," Nico curses as we get closer.

Two men, throats slit, lie on the ground in puddles of long-dried blood. They've been killed hours ago, it seems.

"Goddamnit," I curse under my breath and the back door is broken, hanging off its hinges. We rush inside and there's Alonzo Gallo, one of the Gallo cousins, sitting at the kitchen table with five bullets in his chest, his brown eyes wide and staring.

"Someone got here before we did," Leo says, sounding utterly disappointed.

It could have been anyone, really, because the Gallos are universally hated. Ever since Vincenzo's old man died, he's been running the show in the snakiest way possible, and everyone in the city hates him.

But I think I have an idea of who it might be.

We make our way to Vincenzo's old office upstairs and the house is dead silent. It feels like the very air is dead, and I can smell blood.

There's another two dead bodies in the foyer, shot through the back of the head, execution style.

There's one more on the stairs, his neck broken and hanging at a disturbing angle.

As we step over the last body, Nico's still got his gun out, just in case, but I don't bother. I can tell that it's over.

Nico heads into the office first, kicking the door open, and he gestures for me to come inside.

Romeo Gallo sits in his office chair, shot in the face.

Leo grimaces. "Ugh. Gross," he complains.

Nico doesn't speak, just nudges my arm and gestures to the big family portrait of the Gallos hanging on the wall behind Romeo.

There's a red hourglass emblazoned on the wall, tipped over and spilling sand.

I curse again.

"I should have known Lorenzo would get here first," I mutter.

Leo grumbles something incoherent but Nico sighs heavily, his brows drawn together.

"How many men does Lorenzo have?"

I cock my head, thinking. "I don't know, but from what Mia says, they're a pretty big famiglia."

Nico shakes his head. "I don't know if we stand a chance against Lorenzo and his men if they can cut down this many people in a mansion without even alerting the cops."

"Hey," Leo complains, but I hold my hand up to shut him up.

"Nico's right," I say firmly. "We'll have to play the long game."

"You keep *saying* that," Leo whines and Nico punches him in the arm.

"Who's the *capo*, huh? Dante or you?" Nico taunts.

Leo shuts up.

I'll just have to find another way. I hate myself for not doing it the other night, for not taking care of it. But if he'd been willing to let me in his house alone, without any men or staff, he'll be willing to do it again.

Thing of it is, after the conversation we'd had at dinner and the impressive way he's taken out the Gallos, if I hadn't been planning to kill him for months, I may have liked the man.

I'll bide my time, figure out how to do it the easiest, cleanest way, to save Mia as much stress as I can.

Then I'll take care of it, once and for all, no matter how guilty I might feel about Mia.

"We better get out of here," Leo suggests, and it's the smartest thing he's said all day.

We walk back to the car, put away the guns and go to a local diner, ordering some greasy burgers and fries.

"So, when are you going to do it?" Leo asks.

"You fucking bulldog," Nico complains. "I'm so tired of hearing you bitch about this."

"I'm going to do it when it's the right time," I tell Leo, and he stares at me.

"Is this about that pretty daughter of his?" he asks.

"She's my wife," I snarl, giving him a warning look.

"In name only, right? That's what you said, Dante."

I roll my shoulders, annoyed. "It's none of your business."

"Luca Lorenzo killed your father," Leo says under his breath, in a low tone so no one can hear us.

"Shut your stupid mouth," Nico says, knocking his shoulder against his. "We're in public, you idiot."

Leo shuts up, but I'm irritated because he's right.

I've been putting off killing Luca because of Mia and for no other reason. I've been daydreaming about killing him for months, ever since my father was killed.

I know that I've lost sight of what matters, but I'm conflicted.

"I'll get it done. Don't you worry," I say to Leo, and take a big bite of my burger, hoping he'll let it go.

He gives me a wary look but keeps his mouth shut, thank God.

"You're right to be careful, *capo*," Nico says in a low voice, and he's not a man that often worries, so I'm a little afraid to see the concern on his face.

Have I bitten off more than I can chew?

When Alberto comes back from the bathroom I'm about to exit the door, on the phone, trying to call my dad. He isn't answering and I'm panicking.

Alberto makes a grunt in the back of his throat and shuts the door as I open it, shaking his head and blocking me from exiting the door.

"You're going to let me leave this house," I tell him firmly. "Alone."

He shakes his head again and I look at him for a long moment before I bolt toward the back door. Alberto chases me, but I'm light on my feet and I make it there before him.

He grabs me around the waist, hurting my ribs, and I kick and scream, dragging my new nails across Alberto's forearm.

He hisses as they break the flesh and lets me go.

I run toward the car and make it just as he's trying to open the passenger side door. I burn rubber pulling out of the garage, my head spinning, heart racing.

I feel sick to my stomach. I don't know what to do. Do I go to find Dante, or go straight to my father?

If I go to my father, he's likely to have Dante killed. Maybe I should want that for the way that he's hurt me, but I don't. God help me, I'm still in love with him. My vision blurs out as I'm driving and I swerve, sniffling, trying to get myself together.

But then sobs start catching in my throat and I can't stop them. I pull over on the side of the road, resting my forehead against the steering wheel. Alberto will be right behind me, but I don't care. I can't seem to stop sobbing.

I know that Dante didn't originally marry me for love, but I thought he'd grown to love me. I thought that we'd grown to love each other, and I've never felt so heartbroken.

Instead of Alberto driving up, though, it's Dante in his sportscar and I throw the car back into gear when he gets out of the car, some part of me wanting to run him down, suddenly so angry I can barely see straight.

Instead, though, he puts both hands on the car hood and I can't do it, turning off the car and covering my face, crying into my hands.

Dante gets in the passenger seat.

"Mia, what's wrong? What happened?" he asks, and I hitch in a sob and look at him, tears streaming down my face. Something in his face softens and he puts out a hand to touch me.

I wrench away from him.

"Don't you fucking touch me," I say hoarsely, and Dante looks stricken.

"What's going on, Mia?"

"You don't love me," I sob. "You've never loved me and you never will."

"Mia, what are you *talking* about?"

"Don't play dumb with me, Dante. I know now why you

married me. I know that you just wanted to get close to my father, so you can kill him!"

"Mia..." he starts.

"Did you ever feel anything for me?"

Dante's quiet for a long moment and I shove him. Anger flashes across his face.

"How could I?" he snaps back, every word from his mouth shattering my heart. "How could I ever love you when I know what your father did?"

I just stare at him, shell-shocked. He's finally admitted it, but all that happens is that I feel a void in my chest, like he's ripped my heart out.

Dante takes in a deep breath. "He killed my father, Mia. Both my parents. What am I supposed to do? Just let that go?"

His words rush over me in a wave. All this time, he thought that my father killed his. I stare at him and the tears just keep coming.

"It wasn't my father who killed Enzo. Or your mother," I say quietly.

Dante scoffs, looking away from me, breathing hard. "You don't know that. You just want to believe the best about your father, but he's as cut-throat as any other wiseguy."

"I don't doubt that," I say quietly, slowly beginning to feel numb. I guess I can't feel that depth of emotion for very long without shutting down. I wipe tears from my face. "But when Vincenzo kidnapped me, I overheard his men talking about how Vincenzo would kill you like he did your parents."

"No, you didn't," Dante says, going pale.

"Yes, I did. I didn't tell you because you were injured and I didn't want you to go off and kill Vincenzo and all his men," I say calmly. I'm done with this conversation. Dante lied to me, over and over, the whole time we were together.

"You didn't tell me," Dante whispers.

I shrug, wiping the last of the tears off my face. "Enzo and my father became friends later in life, I thought you knew that. I thought you knew that they were going up against the Gallos together."

"I didn't know," Dante says desperately, his hazel eyes searching my face.

I keep my face blank. "Now you know. So kindly, get out of my car."

"Mia, wait, please—" Dante starts, but I shove him again.

"Get the fuck out of my car!" I nearly scream, and Dante slowly gets out of the passenger seat.

Before he can start to speak, I take off, tires burning, leaving him there, standing, his shoulders slumped.

It seems to take forever to make it to my father's house, and all I can do is burst in the door and run to his office, climbing into his lap like a little girl.

"Mia," my father murmurs, not asking any questions, just pulling me into his arms, letting me sob into his chest. "Cara mia."

"Papa," I hiccup.

He doesn't push me. Doesn't ask any questions, just holds me until my tears slow.

"If you're still afraid about the Gallos, you shouldn't be. Papa took care of it," he soothes, rubbing my back.

I pull away and look at him, the hint of a weak smile pulling at the corner of my mouth. Dante was right about one thing – my father is just as cut-throat as any other wiseguy when it comes to the people he loves.

I can't believe that Dante never cared about me. I can't

believe I let myself believe that he would fall in love with me, if I just loved him enough. Now I'm stuck alone with a bun in the oven.

"Papa," I say softly. "I need to move back home."

Papa frowns, looking down at me. "Did Dante hit you?"

I shake my head. "No, nothing like that."

"Good. I didn't want to have to kill him," my father says, clearly joking, but given everything, I don't find it very funny. I force a weak smile anyway.

"We just have irreconcilable differences," I say softly.

Papa nods. "Your mother and I had that, too," he says. "A few times."

I can't help but chuckle even though my voice is shaky. "You're going to be a grandfather," I say quietly, so quietly that Papa blinks and cups my chin in his hand to get me to look at him.

"What did you say, *cara mia*?"

"You're going to be a grandfather," I say again, my voice stronger.

"Oh," my father breathes, and hugs me tightly, tears forming in his eyes. "Oh, Mia, that's so wonderful."

I sniffle, hugging him back tightly, still cradled in his lap, and wish that I could believe it's wonderful, too. Maybe one day, I will. One day, when Dante is out of my life forever.

29

DANTE

I'm not one of those guys that usually drowns my troubles in alcohol. I like to keep my wits about me, even at parties, but tonight, I feel like I need a bottle of whiskey to quiet the demons in my head.

Nico's in the car with me when I get the text from Alberto about Mia, about how she took off like a bat out of hell. I had gotten to her as quickly as possible, but fat lot of good that did me.

She hates me, and who wouldn't? I had plotted to kill her father, married her just to get close to him. She's got all the reason in the world to hate me, to never talk to me again.

"We're calling off the hit," I say woodenly when I get into the car with Nico, driving toward the mansion.

"What? What are you talking about?" Nico asks incredulously.

"It wasn't him. It was Vincenzo," I say flatly. "Mia told me she overheard them talking."

Nico stares out the window, his face drawn and pale. "Shit. That makes sense, Dante. Gallo and Enzo were on the outs when he was killed."

"I know," I say, my heart wrenching in my chest. If I had thought it through, just for a few days, if I had allowed myself to *think* about it instead of just acting, I would have known that. Instead, I blamed Luca and married Mia.

Do I regret it? No. I don't regret any second that I spent with Mia, but I regret not understanding what really happened. I regret not doing my due research and blaming Luca, and by proxy, Mia, for everything that happened.

"She knows, doesn't she?" Nico asks quietly, and I just nod, feeling like there's a rock stuck in my throat. "What do we do now?"

"I don't know about you," I say quietly, "but I'm going to drink until I can't think anymore."

Nico looks at me for a moment and then nods slowly. "I'll keep an eye on everything for a couple of days."

"Thank you, Nico," I say earnestly, and to my horror, tears burn at the backs of my eyes. I reach the mansion quickly. Nico gets out of the car and walks in with me. Alberto's standing there, looking stressed out, and I wave my hand at him.

"It's okay," I assure him. "I found her."

He doesn't ask any questions, doesn't scribble on his notepad, and I'm grateful. I don't think I can explain the whole thing to him.

Nico follows me into the den where the liquor cabinet is and I pull out a bottle of aged whiskey, the one my father had given me for my birthday before he died.

I had planned on only opening it when I killed Luca, when I finally avenged him, but now...

"Is that the one your old man gave you?" Nico asks.

I nod. "No reason not to open it now," I say, popping open the top and taking a swig directly from the bottle.

"Jesus," Nico curses. "Pour me a glass, would you?"

I do as he says, sliding it to him across the bar where he sits across from me. I remain standing and drinking from the neck of the bottle.

"You've fallen in love with her, haven't you?" Nico asks quietly, and I just look at him for a long moment.

"Yes," I answer in a hoarse whisper.

"Fuck me," Nico says conversationally. "Never thought I'd see the day."

I shrug and drink another long swig. The burn in my throat makes me feel slightly better. "Doesn't matter now, does it?"

"You don't think she'll forgive you?"

I scoff. "How could she? I married her just to get close enough to kill her father."

"It turned into more than that," Nico says and it's not a question. "I've seen how you look at her. How she looks at you. You're like her whole world, Dante."

The words spear through me like a knife, hurting more than a weapon through my skin ever could, and I should know, with all the scars on my body.

"What are you going to do?" Nico asks.

"Nothing," I snort. "What *can* I do?"

"Apologize, you idiot," Nico says disdainfully, giving me a judgmental look. "You can talk to her, tell her that you're sorry. Tell her that you love her."

"She'll never believe me," I say miserably, taking another drink and sitting down hard on the other end of the bar, a couple seats away from Nico. The alcohol is finally kicking in, but as numb as it's making my mouth and throat, my chest still aches.

"You're not even going to try?" Nico asks.

"Would you?" I ask.

Nico shrugs. "Hell, I don't know. I've never been in love, not really."

"I fucking hate it," I admit in a mumble, looking at the quarter-empty bottle in front of me. "It's like your heart is walking around outside your chest."

He whistles. "You got it bad, *capo*."

"You don't know the half of it," I complain. "It's like all I ever do is think about her. Even before I thought about the mission, it was about her."

"I hate to say this, *capo*, but maybe revenge isn't the best thing to pin your whole future on."

"Vincenzo's dead," I say flatly. "I let Luca kill him. I should have done it myself."

"It wouldn't have made you feel any better about Enzo's death," Nico says gently. "What's done is done, and at least the person who killed your parents is gone."

I feel empty, like there's a void in my chest and stomach, and I don't know if it's because Luca killed Vincenzo or because Mia is gone. The emotions swirling around inside of me are all mixed together: guilt, rage, pain, disbelief.

"Get drunk today; go talk to her tomorrow," Nico suggests.

I nod slowly, but I don't know what I will even say to Mia. "*Sorry I plotted to kill your father and married you under false pretenses, baby, but I love you now.*"

She'll probably shove me again, maybe hit me across the face. I deserve it. I deserve worse.

I manage to finish half the bottle of whiskey before I'm lurching to the bathroom and throwing up alcohol and all my negative emotions, flushing the toilet with a grimace before washing my face, swaying in front of the mirror.

Nico is right. I'd bet my whole future on revenge, on

killing the man who killed my father, and I hadn't even thought about what comes next.

"I decided to choose life over death. Love over hate."

I remember Luca's words viscerally, and it's like I finally understand what he was talking about. Even though I was plotting to kill the man, those words had made me pause, even then, and now I understand.

He means that he chose to love someone over hate someone else. He chose his wife and daughter instead of the lifestyle.

I've done the opposite. I've chosen the life instead of Mia, over and over again, despite how I feel about her.

"Do you still need a babysitter?" Nico asks as I stumble back to the couch in the den.

I shake my head, lying down on the couch face-down. "Just gonna take a nap," I slur, and that's the last thing I remember.

When I wake up, I'm lying face-down on the floor instead of the couch, and my shoulder aches where I've fallen off the couch. I ignore it and pick myself up, holding myself up on my desk. On top of it is a wrinkled envelope. It's the autopsy report I'd put on my jacket pocket almost a week ago. With everything going on, I'd forgot about it.

I was waiting for this to be sure, to validate my need for revenge. Now, it's just an envelope. It means nothing. The only thing that means anything to me is gone.

I need Mia. My home. I miss her so much.

Stashing the envelope in my pocket, I decide to go to her, not even bothering to shower or wash my face. It's nearly six in the morning and the sun is starting to rise when I go out to my car.

I need to find Mia. It's the only thing in my hungover

brain, and I need to figure it out. I need to find her before it's too late, before she hates me forever.

I know exactly where to find her.

Luca comes to the door instead of the staff or Mia, and I swallow hard, wondering if she's told him the whole story. I wonder if he'll shoot me right on the doorstep.

His face is blank. "Let me go and get her," he says gruffly, and I let out a sigh of relief.

Mia comes stalking out of the house just a moment later and she pushes me off the step. I stumble backwards, my head still spinning from all the whiskey I've ingested.

"Please," I ask her quietly. "Just hear me out."

She crosses her arms over her chest. "What can you possibly say to make this better, Dante?"

I swallow hard. "I don't know. I don't know but I have to say it."

I look at her and she looks at me, and it seems like there are a thousand miles between us.

30

MIA

I hate the way I'm feeling. My heart aches just looking at Dante, at the bags under his eyes, how he smells like whiskey. He hasn't taken care of himself and he's favoring his injured shoulder. It's stiff while the other is slumped.

So much of me just wants to go to him, wants to wrap my arms around him and just start sobbing into his chest, tell him how much he hurt me.

But my pride won't let me.

"Well, you wanted to talk," I say sharply. "Do it."

"I should have chosen life over death. I should have chosen love over hate," he says, and I blink at him.

"What the hell are you talking about?"

He runs a hand through his hair. "It's something your father said to me," he admits. "He said that when you were small, he was gone all the time. He didn't know how to not choose the lifestyle." Dante takes a step closer and I back toward the open door.

He sighs, holding his hands up as if in defense. "God, Mia, I just want to touch you," he says hoarsely. "I want to take you in my arms and tell you how sorry I am. Will you let me?"

I'm trembling. I shake my head. "No," I say, and I mean to say it firmly but my voice cracks. "No, Dante. Do you have any idea how much you hurt me?"

Dante winces. "I'm so sorry, Mia. I'm sorry, baby," he says earnestly, and it's hard to keep eye contact with him without bursting into tears.

"Sorry isn't going to cut it, Dante."

"I know," he says. "I know that. It's just that I was so determined to find my father's killer. I was just so sure that it was Luca...but now that I'm thinking it through, I know that you were telling me the truth. The Gallos had beef with my father just before he died. I know that it makes more sense that it was Gallo."

"So then *why?*" I ask incredulously. "Why is it that you believed my father did it?"

"They've been rivals forever, and it seemed suspicious that they became friends," he tries to explain, but then shakes his head. "I guess I pinned it on him without much evidence, just wanted to know who did it and settled on him."

"Not only did you want to kill my father, but you married me under false pretenses," I say shakily, anger rising in me. "You told me you wanted me, Dante."

"I do want you, Mia," he explains, putting his hands in his pockets. As he does, his face shows surprise, and he takes out an envelope.

"Here." He holds it out to me, taking another step closer.

"What is this?" I take the envelope but don't open it. It is still sealed.

"My dad's autopsy report. It will tell us if the bullet was a match to other crimes, which would be proof enough of who actually did it... But I don't care anymore. I don't want to know. You know why?"

I can only shake my head.

"Because I decided to choose life. I decided to choose love."

He reaches for me and I don't back up this time, just standing my ground, but I'm still shaking all over.

"You still haven't said it," I whisper. "You've never said it."

Dante searches my face, his own conflicted brows drawn together.

"I'm in love with you, Mia," he says, so quietly I think I must be dreaming.

"What?"

"I'm in love with you," he says again, his voice louder, stronger. "I don't know when it happened, baby, but I fell so hard for you. You're all I think about. You're all I *want* to think about. I choose you."

I'm losing my resolve and I know it. I can't help but drop my arms, opening myself up. Dante takes another step closer, pushes my auburn hair out of my face.

I turn my face into his hand, my heart feeling like it might burst.

"You're not lying this time?" I whisper.

Dante shakes his head fiercely. "I'm not lying. I swear I'm not, pretty girl."

I let him put his arms around me and I sob into his chest, wetting his shirt. He croons sweet nothings to me, soothing me, and eventually, I stop crying and pull away.

"I don't forgive you," I say flatly, and Dante looks crushed, his face falling. "But goddamnit, I *love* you, Dante. I've loved you since I was a teenager."

His eyes shoot to mine, hope flaring in their depths. "You mean that?"

"I've only told you a hundred times," I say, frustrated, and Dante barks out a short laugh.

"Does that mean that you're not going to divorce me?" he asks quietly.

I shrug. "I don't know. Seems like a lot of work."

Dante breaks into a grin. "Yeah, so much work," he agrees.

"But you're not going to get my trust back easily," I say firmly.

"Of course not. I'm willing to do anything, baby. Anything," he promises.

I look at him, into his hazel eyes, and I still feel just as much love as always. I can't let him go, no matter what he's done, what he planned to do.

"No more plotting to kill my father," I say, and Dante laughs softly, his arms still loose around my waist.

"Cross my heart," he says, still smiling.

I slowly smile back, although it's shaky. "You really love me?"

"I really do," he breathes. "So much, Mia. I love you so much."

I burst into tears again and Dante holds me close. "Can we go back home?" he asks in a small voice, and I want to say yes but I'm not sure I can, not yet.

"Not just yet," I say.

Dante pouts, but he doesn't seem offended.

"Go home and shower," I say, wrinkling my nose. "And then you're coming to a family dinner tonight."

Dante blanches. "Only if you promise Luca isn't going to kill me."

"I'd never let him do that," I scold, and then Dante

kisses me, suddenly, and I can't help moaning into his mouth as he sticks his tongue between my lips.

"What time?" he asks against my mouth.

"Eight," I tell him, and back away. He slowly and reluctantly lowers his hands from my hips and nods.

"I'll be here. With bells on," he says.

"You better be," I say, but I can't keep the smile off my face.

Dante does a silly little bow, and I wipe at my face, watching him leave before I walk back into the house.

My father is already smiling at me, standing in the foyer. "Did you reconcile your differences?" he asks.

"Not yet," I say, but I think we have. I think now I can start the road to forgive him.

"Good," he says. "Just like me and your mother."

I take his arm and lead him back into the office. "He's coming for dinner tonight."

My father nods, and I spend the rest of the day napping in my room. When I wake, it's nearly seven, and I feel oddly nervous about dressing for dinner.

I finally settle on a simple, white sundress that looks a lot like the one I wore to my wedding reception. This is a starting over of sorts, anyway, so it seems right.

I'm nervous about dinner although I know the chef's veal lasagna is phenomenal, and I keep going into the kitchen so much that she pushes me out of there, fussing at me in Italian.

I huff and sit down at the table.

Dante shows up at fifteen minutes until eight and speaks to my father at the door.

"I'm sorry about everything, Luca," he says quietly, and Papa raises an eyebrow.

"Shouldn't you be saying that to Mia?"

I scramble into the foyer, trying to signal Dante that I haven't told my father, that he doesn't have to...

"I was plotting to kill you," Dante says flatly, and my father blinks at him.

"You were what now?"

"I thought that you killed my parents," Dante says quietly, keeping eye contact.

My heart is in my throat. My father is a reasonable man, but this is a lot, and I don't know how he's going to react. I brace myself to run in between them so Papa can't hurt him, but instead, my father bursts out laughing.

"Enzo was my best friend," he says. "I would never have hurt him."

Dante smiles slightly. "I was mistaken, Luca, and for that, I'm sorry," he says firmly.

Papa reaches out and pulls him into a hug, patting his back. "Come to dinner, Dante," he says, and that's all the forgiveness that passes between them.

Dante sits next to me, gingerly putting his hand on my knee, as if he's afraid I'll pull away.

I lean against him, putting my head on his shoulder, and I can feel him relax all over.

"I heard that you're giving us a grandchild," Papa says, and Mama joins him, sitting next to him and picking the peas off his plate.

Dante smiles broadly. "I can't wait to meet them," he says softly, and my heart seems to swell. Dante has really come around about the baby, and he's admitted that he loves me.

We all have dinner like a real family, like a real Italian family should be, and I think that Dante's been missing that, having lost his father. He laughs out loud, sounding free and happy, and it's probably the brightest I've ever seen him.

When dinner is over, Dante asks me again.

"Will you come home with me, pretty girl?"

This time, I can't say no. I kiss my father goodbye and hug my mother, and head back home with Dante.

"Should I take the guest room?" he asks quietly when we arrive home, and I shake my head furiously.

When we make love, it's intimate and he's cupping my face with his hands, looking down into my eyes.

When he enters me, he whispers, "I love you, Mia," and it's everything I've always wanted to hear come from his mouth.

"I love you, too," I whisper, tears slipping from my eyes from all the emotions, and Dante takes his thumbs and wipes them away, still moving inside me.

When I come, I clutch at him, digging my nails into his back. I'm making marks that I hope will sting in the shower, make him remember me later.

Dante groans loudly when he spills inside me, kissing along my neck, the side of my face.

"You can't ever leave me again," he says fiercely. "It was awful without you."

I laugh. "It was only twenty-four hours, Dante."

"Too long," he mumbles, pulling out of me with a wince and sliding into bed next to me.

I run my fingers along the marks I've made on his back, his shoulders. "Too long," I admit.

I still haven't completely forgiven him. I'm still hurt, but now that I know he loves me, things are different.

I know there's a long way to go, but I think everything will be all right.

31

DANTE

Luca and Anastasia come to our house for Thanksgiving the next year, after we all go to Mass together. They immediately make their way up to the nursery, where little Alessia is sleeping peacefully. We haven't all gotten together since the baby was born, and so her grandparents are eager to see her.

Anastasia picks her up, waking her, but Alessia only smiles broadly at her. At six months old, she's smiling and laughing all the time.

She's my happy, sweet little *bella*, and I only thought my feelings for Mia were strong. What I feel for this little baby is indescribable. I'd move heaven and earth to make her happy, make them *both* happy, and I plan to.

It took some time for Mia to forgive me. We spent days talking, nights making love, like we should have done in the beginning. I was completely honest with her, and she with me, and eventually, we got to a better place.

I do some of the side dishes for Thanksgiving dinner, but I do let Marisa do most of the cooking. She's the chef in the family, after all, although I do like to cook.

The turkey is delicious and moist and the roasted potatoes I've made as a side are a huge hit. And of course, there's homemade pasta, ziti, and manicottis, and everyone eats their fill.

Nico and Alberto are there, too, shoveling down food with various moans and compliments, and Mia giggles at them. We don't have to worry about taking turns holding the baby like usual, because Anastasia won't let her go.

I look at three generations of beautiful women and smile, taking a mental picture. I already spoil Mia and Alessia relentlessly, and Luca does too. Mia keeps warning me that she'll be a little brat, but I don't care.

I fully admit that my girls have me wrapped around their little fingers.

We have something to tell Alessia's grandparents, too, and Mia smiles at me as I sit next to her. She intwines her fingers with mine, resting them on my thigh.

"We have some news," she starts, and Anastasia says something quickly to Mia in Russian.

Mia laughs and nods, and Anastasia bursts into tears.

Luca looks at me, confused, and I shrug, also looking confused.

"We're having another baby," I explain to him as Anastasia gets up and hugs Mia tightly.

"Irish twins," Luca chuckles.

"Not quite. The baby won't be born until April. Let's call them Italian twins," I correct, and he barks out another laugh. He looks at his wife and daughter and granddaughter just as fondly as I do before turning back to me.

"Are you happy with your choice, Dante?" Luca asks quietly while the girls are occupied.

I smile brightly. "It's the best choice, Luca. You were right."

He nods slowly, and I can't explain the happiness I feel, how bright everything seems now that my quest for vengeance is over and Mia and Alessia are in my life.

"Are you happy, Dante?" Mia asks me, looking at me curiously, as if she's worried that another child might make me panic.

"I never knew what happiness was before I married you," I say, and I mean it. It had always been just another couple of nights with a woman, another few days with my family. I've never thought about my future, not in any real way that didn't involve death and hate.

Mia has taught me what real life is, what real love is, and I never want to let her go.